Journey's End

Dora Hiers

Journey's End

All scripture quotations, unless otherwise indicated, are taken from the Holy Bible, New International Version[R], NIV[R], Copyright 1973, 1978, 1984 by Biblica, Inc.™ Used by permission of Zondervan. All rights reserved worldwide. www.zondervan.com

Cover Art by *Kim Mendoza*

White Rose Publishing, a division of Pelican Ventures, LLC
www.whiterosepublishing.com
PO Box 1738 *Aztec, NM * 87410

White Rose Publishing Circle and Rosebud logo is a trademark of Pelican Ventures, LLC

Publishing History
First White Rose Edition, 2011
Print Edition ISBN 978-1-61116-080-2
Electronic Edition ISBN 978-1-61116-081-9
Published in the United States of America

Dedication

To my precious Heavenly Father. Thank you for not allowing me to give up and for holding my hand during the journey.

To my awesome husband. Thank you for always believing in me, for encouraging me when I needed it, and for holding my other hand.

To my editor, Jamie West. Thank you for your timing in sharing such wonderful news with me. What a great way to start the new year!

1

The mystery man with haunted eyes was back.

Chelsea Hammond placed the lawn chairs next to the cooler in the trunk, but kept her eyes on the man. He stood alone, farther up the hill, tucked under some towering maple trees. Far enough away that she couldn't make out all his features, but close enough for Chelsea to glimpse his pain. The slight slumping of his expansive shoulders; the hands clenched at his sides; the haunted eyes that stared out into the distance when he removed his sunglasses; the lips set in a straight, hard line.

And the words "Deputy U.S. Marshal" that blazed from the front of his polo shirt. It had taken her three years, but this year she determined to talk to him, to rid her dreams of those haunted eyes. To hear his story. To offer closure if his version somehow connected to hers.

Chelsea closed the trunk of the old Cadillac and turned to her in-laws. "There you go, Henry. You're all set."

"Thank you, dear. We appreciate you lugging those lawn chairs for us." Henry opened the door for his wife while she wrestled to get into the car, sweat beading on her upper lip. Henry and Stella always made a day of it when they visited their two sons.

"You're welcome. You take it easy going home."

Chelsea peered overhead at the steely gray clouds, swirling into angry puffs. "Looks like a storm is brewing."

Henry followed her gaze, and then turned to look at her. "Oh, we will, dear. We don't have far to go. Will we see you next year?"

Her stomach lurched. She couldn't let Doug's elderly parents face this day alone. Besides, where else would she be on the anniversary of her husband's death? "Same time, same place, Henry." Chelsea smiled and leaned into the car to give Stella a peck on her moist cheek. "Bye, Stella."

Chelsea straightened and Henry wrapped his frail arms around her for a hug. "Glad to see you with a smile on your face this year."

She slipped away from his embrace, blinking, until Henry started the engine. The giant sedan glided away, their hands flapping through the open windows. She lifted her hand in return, the smile still firmly planted across her lips. Henry was right. This was the first year she hadn't cried on his shoulder.

Thunder rumbled across the sky, and she jumped, feeling the echo vibrate against the ground. Fat raindrops splashed against her bare legs.

She glanced up the hill. The mystery man was gone.

Disappointment sliced through her chest. Maybe next year.

Chelsea hurried towards her truck and dived in through the open door. Now she wished she'd taken the time to change from her sundress into jeans after the graduation ceremony this morning.

She exited the memorial gardens and headed south on the interstate towards Charlotte. Dark gray clouds dumped rain from the sky, but even the stormy skies couldn't dampen her spirits. Her sunglasses and an unopened tissue box sat on the seat next to her. She dared a glance in the rear-view mirror. Nope. Not bloodshot. Wonder blossomed in her chest.

Life was turning around. Finally.

She hunched forward and strained to see, the windshield wipers swishing at their maximum speed, her white knuckles gripping the steering wheel. She slowed down to exit the interstate and released a pent-up breath.

She pulled to a stop in front of the barn and cut the engine. Two streaks of lightning pierced the sky, snapping into electrical balls a few feet away. She sucked in a deep breath and pulled the keys from the ignition, chuckling at her shaky hands.

Thunder couldn't be too far behind.

One-thousand-one, one-thousand-two, one-thousand-three. A long crack of thunder boomed through the silence, the ground trembling in its wake.

Whew. That was close.

Chelsea waited, peering through the rain pelting the windshield, feeling the truck sway with the heavy winds. She didn't want to go out in this, but she had to check on Molly. Kalyn, her live-in housekeeper, had fed the fawn earlier but Chelsea wanted to settle her in for the night. Besides, this rain didn't appear to be lessening. She couldn't stay in the truck all night.

She glanced to the passenger seat, deciding to leave her purse in the truck for now. She reached under the seat for the umbrella. She couldn't use it now, but maybe the rain would dwindle enough where she could use it from the barn to the house. She slipped her sandals off. No need to ruin them.

Jerking the door open, she bolted for the barn, gripping her sundress, the wind all but whipping it over her head. Good thing it was just her and Kalyn out here.

She reached the barn and screeched to a halt, digging toes in the wet grass. The door stood slightly ajar. Alarm snaked up and down Chelsea's spine. Hadn't she closed it when she left this morning? She knew she had. She'd been worried about Molly roaming around, so she'd locked her up in a stall. A baby deer without a mama was easy prey.

Chelsea shook her head. Enough. Wondering wasn't keeping her dry. She slid the barn door open the rest of the way and stepped inside. Mustiness and humidity slammed her in the face, along with the comfortable smells of leather and hay. Chelsea flipped on the light switch, but nothing happened.

She squeezed back the apprehension that rippled through her chest. The storm had clearly knocked out the power; she'd seen the fireballs.

Water rolled down the middle of her back. She shook her head, bouncing wet curls to get some of the water off, and then gathered long hair in her hands and squeezed. That would have to do until she got inside where she had access to a dry towel. She shivered and rubbed her upper arms to generate some warmth.

Her eyes adjusted to the darkness. OK, so the barn smelled normal, but something didn't *feel* right. Chelsea scanned the cool interior. The riding lawn mower and a few garden tools. Some extra straw for Molly's stall. Looked about the same as it did every other day.

She was acting like a baby. She needed to get over

it. Kalyn had probably come out to feed Molly, and then left the door open. End of story.

Chelsea gritted her teeth and pushed shoulders back. She wasn't scared. She couldn't be. When Journey's End opened next week, a bunch of teenagers would look to her as a role model for strength and courage. Teenagers could sense cowardice. They wouldn't see it in her. No way.

Rain pummeled the barn roof. The wind howled, screaming through the open door of the barn and hurling straw pieces from one wall to the other. Another deafening crack of thunder boomed outside. She jumped, a nervous giggle escaping from her throat.

So, maybe she was just a little scared. She'd feel better if she were inside the house sipping a cup of coffee. Something to warm up her insides.

She would check on Molly. Get inside and dry off. Then whip up the latest recipe for apple pie that she'd been dying to try. Oh yeah. She grinned. Sounded good.

With quick steps, she headed towards Molly's stall and pulled the latch to open the gate.

A streak of lightning flashed from the open door, lighting up the inside of the barn, and she turned to look outside. Blinded, Chelsea blinked and waited for her eyes to readjust, expecting to see Molly cowering in the corner.

But she didn't. Molly snuggled comfortably next to something.

Someone?

Chelsea gasped, hearing the wild pounding of her pulse over the rain hammering on the roof.

A pencil-thin teenager scrambled to his knees, grabbing something from the straw next to him. Drool oozed from his open mouth, and straw poked out of his black hair. With sleepy brown eyes, he crouched on one knee and brandished a pitch fork at her like it was a rifle. "Don't co-come any cl-closer."

Chelsea did what any rational female would have done under the circumstances.

She screamed and threw hands in the air, the umbrella banging against her forearm.

He frowned and shook his head. "I...I'm not go-going to hurt you, lady." Squeaky Voice said. He brushed the lone tear sliding down one cheek with his shirt sleeve. "I wouldn't."

"I believe you." Chelsea took a step closer. The umbrella zinged open. *Whoosh.*

Chelsea rolled her gaze to the open umbrella and then back to the teenager.

Surprise distorted Squeaky Voice's face until he dropped the pitchfork to the straw and doubled over, laughing. He laughed like he couldn't imagine a tomorrow, like he couldn't bear to look at yesterday, like he didn't want to face today. Tears streamed down his face.

She knew that laugh. Recognized the tears.

Shock.

She needed to get him inside and assess the situation. She lowered her hands, slow and easy, and tossed the umbrella into the corner of the stall. She held out a hand with more confidence than she felt. "I'm Chelsea Hammond. Welcome to Journey's End."

He waited a few beats before standing up to his full six foot plus height. In what seemed like slow motion, his hand slid into hers. "I'm Jacob Carpocelli."

Her stomach threatened to give up the hamburger she had devoured on the drive home. The stall started to spin. She reached out with a hand to steady herself against the door. Maybe she was the one who would need medical attention. "Did you say Jacob *Carpocelli*?"

He nodded while his face blanched, almost like he didn't want to be known by his last name. She could understand that. Jacob tugged his hand away from her wet, slimy one and stepped back. "Jacob's my real name, but I just go by Jake."

"Jake?" Was that harsh whisper her voice?

Tony Carpocelli's son?

God, why would you do this to me?

OK. Maybe she wasn't so ready for closure after all.

❧

It wasn't too late to turn around.

Yeah, well, maybe it wasn't too late to turn around, but he wouldn't have a job to turn around to. His boss had made that clear.

Trey Colten spotted the end of the snaking road and blew out a long breath. "Looks like we're here. I don't see any signs for the shelter, but this is the right address."

Renner Crossman, his partner, glanced up from studying the case file and looked at him, sympathy oozing from his face. "Sorry about what happened with the chief, buddy."

"Yeah." Trey's hands clenched the steering wheel. He turned into the clearing used for parking, pulling the Suburban to a stop in front of a house tucked deep in the middle of a forest. Hundreds of chirping birds drowned out any noise that might otherwise have filtered through the trees, like the neighbor's dog from two miles back that ran back and forth barking at their car. Good ol' Nowhere, USA.

The chugging of a lawn mower sounded nearby although they couldn't see it.

Hammond's widow?

Trey's gut churned, and he reached in the center console for his roll of antacids, popping one into his mouth with a loud sigh. "Tell me again how Carpocelli's kid found this place."

"Chelsea Hammond's brother."

"Her brother?"

"Yeah, indirectly. It says here that"—Renner flipped the page in the folder to read the notes—"Chelsea's brother is the resource officer at Jake's school."

"Chelsea's brother sent him here?" Trey frowned. What kind of brother would send trouble to his sister in the form of Jake Carpocelli? Trey might go looking for her brother when he got back to Raleigh. Sit down and have a friendly little chat with him. Instruct him on the dos and don'ts of brotherhood. *Do not* send a kid related to the mob to your sister's house.

"No. Her brother didn't *send* him here."

Trey rolled his eyes and opened his door, his legs not cooperating. "So if Chelsea's brother didn't send Jake…"

"Jake was chatting with the resource officer in his office. The officer was called out for a fight."

"Let me guess. He left Jake sitting in his office while he took care of business?"

"Yep. Chelsea's advertising fliers were on his desk."

"Ah. Pretty slick kid." Trey still wanted that chat with the brother. It was due to his negligence that Carpocelli's kid had landed here. That burned his gut.

He popped another antacid in his mouth before stuffing the roll in his pocket.

Renner grinned and opened his door wide. "Let's go, cowboy. Home sweet home."

Trey glared at his partner. Renner's joking manner only set him further on edge. Didn't he know who they were up against? Tony Carpocelli? He wouldn't put anything past that scum. His drug money would buy anything. Or anybody. Trey knew not to trust Carpocelli, even if Carpocelli was locked up, but nobody else seemed inclined to take Trey seriously.

"Maybe it's time for a new partner."

Renner scoffed. "Yeah, right. Nobody else will put up with you like I do."

"I think it's the other way around."

Renner threw his head back and laughed. "Could be. But after your conversation with the chief this morning, I don't think that's happening anytime soon."

Trey gritted his teeth and forced his legs out of the car. "Don't remind me. I should have tendered my resignation. While I still had a job."

Renner walked around the car to join him, his dark eyebrows raised. "Meaning you won't have one after this is over?"

"You never know," Trey mumbled, looking away from the troubled eyes of his partner to scan the yard.

Two other agents were staged at vantage points around the perimeter, but this area was his worry. He wanted to make sure he knew what he was up against before trouble came knocking. And he was fairly sure it would. It was just a matter of time.

His eyes settled on the wrap-around front porch. Water gurgled softly down the side of a ceramic pot. Giant green ferns swayed gently in the breeze. Rocking chairs, Adirondacks and a swinging bench beckoned visitors to step onto the porch, to relax and embrace the solitude, the serenity.

He took a deep breath, appreciating the scent of freshly mowed grass.

This place whispered peace, quiet, and tranquility. He could see how it would be a beacon to a troubled soul. His lips twisted in a grimace. Too bad it had to attract the likes of Carpocelli's son.

Most of the time Trey liked kids. But this was Carpocelli's son. Maybe it was a blessing in disguise that the chief had given him responsibility for the widow.

Trey licked his dry lips.

"Nervous, buddy?" Renner said.

Trey shot him another annoyed glance. "Shove it, Renner."

His gaze jerked back to the front door. Their trip from Raleigh had taken a little over two hours, but now it didn't seem nearly long enough. With his eyes focused on the front door, he took the first step and willed his mind to cooperate. His boots felt weighted down with mud. Renner's movement from behind forced him forward.

He licked his lips again. The widow Hammond would be standing in front of him in about four minutes.

Three years and he still wasn't ready for this. How could he explain the knot in his stomach that grew tighter every time he heard the name Hammond? Like a sucker punch to the belly that produced more pain with every blow.

He had considered quitting after the chief refused to take him off this assignment, even up until he got in the car today. Days like this, he didn't like his job. Where was the justice in all this?

He blinked and shook his head, hoping to clear his thoughts, to shake off this pathetic attitude. An attitude that could get him killed if he wasn't careful.

He slowed his steps further, glanced back at Renner. How could he explain to his partner the sudden, urgent desire to...uh, take an extended vacation? Trey reached the end of the sidewalk and started up the steps. It wasn't too late. They could be in the Suburban and out of here before anybody knew different. But where would they—?

"Looking for Journey's End, gentlemen?"

That wasn't good. She already caught him off guard, and he hadn't even rung the doorbell. How was he ever going to focus on this assignment? He took a deep breath before turning around, hands fisted at his sides.

Renner pushed his back and propelled him forward, but Trey dug his heels in the ground a few feet away from the widow. He'd never seen her this close.

Chelsea Hammond's simple beauty knocked the breath out of his lungs. Curly auburn locks cascaded gently onto a cream-colored shirt, and faded jeans graced gentle curves. Her lips formed a slight smile, and freckles peeked out from under a hint of makeup. A fawn nestled at her side, enhancing her sweetness and gentle aura.

Panic rippled through his chest at the war going on between guilt and attraction. His memories—and he hated to admit—his dreams hadn't captured her essence. He wasn't sure what he expected, but it definitely wasn't the beauty standing in front of him.

Trey tipped his head forward in a slight nod. "Ma'am."

"Good afternoon, gentlemen. I'm Chelsea Hammond. Welcome to Journey's End." She extended her hand, graceful, poised.

And him? He needed to get his act together before he lost his job. Reaching out to shake her hand required all of Trey's willpower. "Trey Colten. Deputy U.S. Marshal." Trey flashed his badge briefly, as he always did.

She tugged her hand from his grasp. Heart racing, he studied her through hooded lids, not wanting his eyes to mirror his own thoughts but wanting, no, needing, to know hers.

Trey tilted his head sideways to introduce Renner, never taking his eyes off Chelsea's face. "And this is my partner, Renner Crossman."

Renner shook hands with Chelsea and flashed his badge.

"Please forgive me, but may I take a closer look at your badges?"

"Sure." Trey reached for Renner's badge and handed both to Chelsea for closer identification. "We appreciate your caution. You're tucked out here in the wilderness pretty far." An understatement for sure. Two miles from her nearest neighbor? The chief had mentioned Chelsea installed a security system specifically designed for the shelter. He made a mental note to ask her about that later.

"Not so far out that Jake couldn't find me, I guess."

She had a point there. He caught her biting her lower lip while she studied the badges, and his stomach clenched. Did she recognize him from her husband's graveside? He visited Hammond's grave every year, around the same time as her, but he always stayed far enough away where she couldn't recognize him.

Or maybe she recognized his name from the newspaper? He'd scoured the newspaper for weeks after Hammond's death, relieved that the Marshal's office hadn't coughed up his name to the press.

She couldn't possibly know him, could she?

Trey stuffed an antacid in his mouth, almost swallowed it whole.

She handed back their badges without a word, and he released the pressure that had been building in his lungs. "I believe you spoke with Joshua Hamilton, our Deputy Supervisor from the Raleigh office who worked out the details of our visit?"

Chelsea nodded.

"Would you mind if we continued this conversation inside?" The hair on the back of Trey's neck stood on end. Standing outside, exposed, made him feel like a sitting duck. A big, open target, screaming, "Shoot me."

Chelsea blinked and her eyes grew wide. "Oh, sure. I'm sorry. Come on in. Do you need me to call Jake in?"

"Let me guess. Jake's the one mowing the lawn?" Renner's voice expressed the disbelief that threatened to clog Trey's arteries.

Jake, their key witness, was outside mowing the lawn? In broad daylight?

"Is there anything sweeter than a teenager mowing the lawn?" Summer and sunshine sparkled in Chelsea's smile. She scooted passed him to wave at Jake, leaving the fawn lazing in the grass. The light scent of jasmine floated around Trey's head.

Trey had anticipated other emotions from Chelsea. Like coldness. Anger. Contempt. Even had prepared himself for hatred. Those he could deal with, would actually make his job easier. But this sweetness and sugar? It would kill him. If one of Carpocelli's thugs didn't get to him first.

Trey waited while their witness, the one they were supposed to be protecting, rumbled over to Chelsea and cut the motor, casting a furtive glance in their direction. Chelsea spoke quietly to Jake before he hopped off the lawn mower. Trey didn't miss the look that passed between them or the way she placed her hand protectively on Jake's back while she led the way indoors.

Trey caught Renner's raised eyebrows and his cocky grin before following Chelsea inside. Once inside the reception area, he allowed his eyes to wander. In the connecting room, sofas and recliners arranged in different settings throughout the massive area beckoned them to relax, and a 52-inch flat screen television played softly over a beautiful stone fireplace. He could imagine the flames frolicking quietly in the fireplace during the winter, adding a touch of warmth to the large room. Balls were racked on a nearby pool table, set and ready, inviting them to play.

Chelsea, still with her hand against Jake's back, propelled them around, her quiet spirit a healing balm. No wonder Jake had found his way to Journey's End.

Maybe there were some perks to staying here after all.

Something about Jake's profile blasted through Trey's consciousness, reminding him of Carpocelli. Did Chelsea know who this kid was? Did she know that

Jake's last name was Carpocelli? As in Tony Carpocelli's son? Tony Carpocelli, the murderer who killed her husband? Why hadn't they thought of asking the chief that important detail?

OK, go with the flow. No sense in giving away Jake's last name or trying to fabricate one at the last minute. He would never be able to keep up with the lie. All the lies.

He could hardly live with the truth.

Trey stuck out his hand. "I'm Trey Colten, and this is Renner Crossman. We're from the U.S. Marshal's office. You must be Jake."

"Yeah." The kid squawked, sliding his sweaty palm into Trey's. Dressed in slim-fitting jeans and a wrinkled t-shirt, Jake didn't come across as a wealthy fourteen-year-old. All the money in the world couldn't help the kid now. He was scared to death. Scared of them? Or retaliation from his father?

Trey would find out eventually. "Jake, I'm sorry about your mother."

"Yeah. Thanks." The kid swiped at his eyes with the back of his arm.

Trey turned his head away to give Jake a chance to pull himself together. "We'll need to sit down and talk with you for a few minutes. Ask you a few questions about what happened and discuss the schedule for the next few weeks."

"Yeah. Sure." Another squawk.

"You guys can make yourselves comfortable in here." Chelsea led them to the seating area in front of the fireplace and then disappeared. Trey sank down into one of the leather recliners and closed his eyes for a moment.

He opened his eyes to see Jake settle on the couch,

his white knuckles gripping the arm, while Renner plunked down in the other recliner.

Trey leaned forward, resting his elbows on his knees. He didn't want to be too comfortable. He had a job to do. "You'll be spending most of your time with Agent Crossman."

Renner grinned at the kid. "Just call me plain old Renner."

"And you can call me Trey."

"OK."

So far so good. "Do you have any specific questions we might be able to answer right now?"

"Do you guys know when my mom's funeral is?"

O-K. That didn't take long to go south. Trey glanced at Renner, hoping he might want to field that question.

Renner took the bait. "It's planned for Monday at two."

"Will I be able to go?" Hopeful brown eyes flicked warily from him to Renner, scanning the two of them for the response he wanted.

Trey measured his answer. Let the kid think about the danger in going to the funeral. "Do you think that would be a wise thing to do?"

Jake's eyes narrowed and filled. "I don't care if it's the wise thing to do. She's my mom."

Trey settled back in the recliner at Jake's sudden hostility and reached for his roll of antacids. He popped one in his mouth.

Chelsea walked into the great room carrying a tray of glasses filled with ice and a full pitcher. She placed the tray on the coffee table and sat down on the couch next to Jake, glancing at the three of them as she poured. "Iced tea?"

"Sure, thanks." Trey reached to take hold of the

glass she offered, and then watched Renner and Jake do the same.

Trey took a sip. Sweet, with just the right amount of sugar. Good stuff.

No one said anything. Chelsea looked up, an uncomfortable expression settling on her face. "I'm sorry. I didn't mean to intrude on this conversation." She started to stand.

Jake stopped her with his free hand. He coughed and seemed to fight to keep control of his emotions. He wasn't winning. "They're trying to tell me that I can't go to my mom's funeral." His voice faltered and then exploded, sorrow making his words sound angry. "My own mother's funeral."

Chelsea's censure flitted from Trey to Renner, leaving both of them aware of how she felt. Mama bear.

"How could there be a problem with Jake attending his mother's funeral?"

A problem? Couldn't she see that attending the funeral would create just a tiny little problem? As in ambush? "You do realize Jake's dad doesn't work by himself? There's probably six or seven guys waiting for word from him, happy to do his dirty work."

He heard her soft intake of breath. So he scared her. Good. Now if he could only scare Jake. "Have either of you considered that Jake's mom's funeral would be the first place one—"

"Maybe you guys would like to freshen up? Give Jake a chance to catch his breath. I believe your rooms are ready." Chelsea interrupted. She stood, pointing towards the stairwell. "If you'll follow me—"

"We have a lot to go over and not much time—" Renner stopped her mid-sentence.

Chelsea flashed her teeth, something between a smile and a warning. "You're at Journey's End now. In our little corner of the world we have all the time we need. Right, Jake?"

2

"Wow. You smell good enough to eat. Which I'm going to do right now."

Chelsea set the pan of brownies on the stovetop and reached for a knife from the drawer. She cut only one little square and popped it in her mouth.

She closed her eyes and moaned. Nothing like chocolate to soothe her frazzled nerves. And they were frazzled today. She'd weathered that awful storm. Survived the wild-haired teenager brandishing a pitchfork. In her job as a guidance counselor, she'd learned that with teenagers, one should always expect the unexpected. They never let one down that way.

She could handle the teens.

It was the marshals she could do without.

"I'm supposed to be the one with a ravenous appetite, Chelsea, not you," Kalyn said, walking through the kitchen into the utility room to stow her tub of cleaning supplies. Chelsea could hear her chuckling.

Kalyn stepped back into the kitchen and bent over the sink to wash her hands.

"Well, since you suffer from morning sickness, I guess it's my job to make up for your lack of appetite." Chelsea finished cutting the rest of the brownies into squares and loaded them into a serving basket.

Kalyn grinned and accepted the brownie that

Chelsea dangled in front of her face. "All the upstairs bedrooms and the bathrooms are finally clean. You're ready for business. Do you need me to do anything else?" Kalyn tore off a chunk and nibbled, actually *nibbled*. Chelsea wanted to snatch it out of her hands and eat it properly.

"No, not at the moment. Hey, thanks for cleaning those rooms on a Friday night."

Kalyn rolled her eyes, typical teenager style. "That's my job, Chelsea, remember?"

"I'm sure cleaning doesn't rank high on the list of things you enjoy doing on your weekend." Chelsea gave the spaghetti sauce on the stove a quick stir.

"Yeah, well, sharing your house with a pregnant, hormonal teenager probably doesn't rank too high on yours, either." Kalyn hung her head and patted her little belly with gentle hands. At three months, she hadn't started showing yet. "I appreciate you letting me stay here, Chelsea, so if I have to clean the entire house from top to bottom on a Friday night, that's what I'll do."

Chelsea slung her arm around Kalyn's shoulders and pulled her close for a hug. "Thanks, Kalyn. I love you, sweetie." Chelsea loosened her hold and stepped back before the tears formed. She didn't want to have bloodshot eyes tonight over the dinner table, so she lightened her voice and changed the subject. "So what's on your agenda tonight? Up for some spaghetti?"

"I saw Jake's condition when he stormed upstairs earlier, what with his red eyes and smoke blasting out of his eardrums. Uh, no thanks." Kalyn grinned, mischief making her green eyes sparkle.

Chelsea laughed. "I can't say that I blame you."

"Actually, I'm babysitting Matt for Jamee and Ethan tonight. They asked me to spend the night because they'll be late. Remember? I told you last week right after they asked."

"Oh, that's right. Their anniversary dinner." Chelsea tapped her index finger against her lower lip. "Hmmm. Maybe you'll need some help with Matt?"

At Kalyn's slow shake of her head, Chelsea laughed and reached for the basket of brownies. "Can't blame a girl for trying, can you? So you'll be back sometime tomorrow morning?"

Kalyn nodded. "They said to tell you not too early. They wanted to sleep in after getting in really late. Ethan's mom's flight doesn't get in until midnight."

"Well, have fun with Matt. I'm off in search of Jake. He needs something to calm his nerves before dinner tonight." A couple brownies wouldn't ruin his appetite, from what she knew already.

Chelsea took tentative steps towards the great room, not sure where Renner and Trey were hiding out. "Jake?"

"In here."

"In here" turned out to be the billiards area off the great room. She found him just as the three ball bounced off the table and landed on the hardwood floor with a loud thud. She winced.

Poor kid. After his sulking episode earlier, he sought her out, sitting at the kitchen counter and talking while she mixed up the brownies. Then he went to the great room and alternated between watching television, getting on the computer, and playing a game of pool. With a zillion trips to the bathroom in between. Probably trying to keep his mind off the next meeting looming with the two agents.

She couldn't blame him. She could use a little distraction, too. Hoisting herself onto the tall pub chair, she held out the plate. "Brownie?"

"Thanks, Chelsea." Jake took one and leaned his back against the pool table while he ate it, swallowing in less bites than it took for her to grab another one of her own. *The last one*, she promised herself.

"Are you worried, Jake?" Nervous? Anxious? Aggravated? She was all of the above. And more, judging by the rocks lining the inside of her stomach. It couldn't be from the dessert.

"Nah." His squeaky voice and lowered head belied his words. He leaned over the pool table, aimed his stick to hit the balls, but the white ball barely tapped the others.

"You did the right thing, sweetie, telling Mr. Hamilton you'd testify against your father."

Brown eyes, filled with too much pain for such a short life, searched for reassurance in hers. Her heart ached for the young man on the hard road to manhood. Too bad he hadn't had a better role model in his life.

"Yeah. I know." He made another shot and missed.

"Are you having second thoughts?"

"No. Third or fourth, maybe, but not second."

She could relate. "Jake, Mr. Hamilton assured me that your father was locked up tight right now. No need to worry."

She was telling the poor kid not to worry. With intricate links to the mob and connections all over the world, did it matter whether the man was in jail or not? She should change the security code tonight, just to be on the safe side.

He only nodded and turned his back to her, replacing his stick on the wall rack.

"If these guys don't treat you right or get on your nerves, you let me know. I'll send them packing."

"You're such a mom, Chelsea. Why don't you have a gazillion kids?"

Her sunny mood faded at his joking words. Jake didn't know. He didn't know the pain his own father had caused *her*. And he didn't know what calling the marshal's office had cost her emotionally. Maybe she would tell Jake when it was all over.

But not now. Carpocelli's son or not, this stuck-somewhere-between-a-boy-and-a-man kid needed her help.

Chelsea's throat closed, and she sputtered. "Well, I...should go finish...up in the kitchen. Dinner won't make it to the table by itself."

Chelsea retreated to the kitchen, where she could busy herself with the finishing touches on dinner. Where she could push back the memories that threatened to overwhelm her.

She prepped the spaghetti for serving, forcing her mind to happier thoughts. Journey's End was finally open, ready or not. Something she'd dreamed about since she was twenty, although the idea had germinated much earlier than that.

Humming, she carried the serving platter into the dining room and set it on the buffet table. She cracked the dining room window open, allowing a gentle breeze to drift through the room, lifting curls from her shoulders. She stood there, peering outside until her eyes focused on the darkened barn.

Oops! She'd forgotten the horses were scheduled to be delivered this weekend. She should call tonight and delay their arrival until next week. No sense in passing off her frazzled nerves to the horses.

If someone had told her a year ago that two marshals would be staying in her house, she would have argued with them. Called them crazy. Her heart skipped a beat, and a huge lump formed in her throat. God definitely had a sense of humor.

Three years. It had taken three years to get to this point. Where she didn't wake up dreading another long day. Three years of praying to forgive the marshal in charge of the undercover operation that took her husband's life. Praying from a distance was one thing, but God had actually dropped two marshals on her doorstep. What was He trying to tell her?

Why, God? Of all the shelters in the world why did Jake end up at mine?

A good working relationship with all government offices would go a long ways towards making her teen shelter successful. She didn't need to be labeled a troublemaker or someone who was difficult to work with.

Chelsea straightened her shoulders, lifted her chin. She could do this. She would do this. For Jake. For other teens like him. For the success of Journey's End.

God, help me be pleasant to these men. I'm sure they're not responsible for Doug's death. They seem nice enough.

She turned away from the window and glanced around the room. Fresh flowers and three place settings of her casual dinnerware adorned the table. Candles flickered on the buffet table, illuminating the dinner offering with a soft glow. Light jazz filtered in quietly from a built-in speaker. She smiled, satisfied with her efforts to create a comfortable, relaxing atmosphere. Jake needed that tonight.

"Wow. Nice spread. I thought I smelled dinner," Renner said, as he walked into the dining room with a huge smile.

Jake trailed close behind Renner, sporting a pasty face and solemn expression. Chelsea smiled and saw his body relax slightly, his face lighten. *Chin up, buddy.*

Trey entered the dining room last, scowling after he glanced at the table.

Chelsea did a quick scan of the room. Had she forgotten something?

"You're not eating with us?" Trey asked.

Was this guy observant or what?

Both men wore dress shirts with ties, but Trey was the most striking. Not so much what he wore. More from his aura of self-confidence, with the straight shoulders, the hard line of his jaw, the slight tilt of his lips.

Whatever. Her work-around-the-house jeans didn't seem appropriate for the dinner table with these two guys. Chelsea shook her head. "I'll eat afterwards; make sure you guys have everything you need. Besides, I didn't have a chance to change my clothes."

Trey inspected her from head to toe, his dark blue eyes shimmering. "You look beautiful just the way you are. You've got everything covered. And we would prefer that you join us. We're really not as bad as you might think."

No. They were worse.

"Please, Chelsea," Jake pleaded.

She became the object of three sets of eyes. Her heart plummeted to her stomach, and a warm flush crept up her neck.

How could she say no? Jake needed her. Chelsea hesitated for only a few seconds before nodding. "OK, then. I'll just be a minute. You guys go ahead." She hurried to the kitchen to retrieve the extra silverware and a plate while Renner and Jake helped themselves from the buffet.

She returned in time to hear the click of the dining room window and Trey pulling the curtains closed. Scooping up his plate, he positioned himself in line behind Jake.

Chelsea pressed her lips into a thin line. "Umm...I just opened that window."

"Oh, I'm sorry. It's getting towards dusk. We'd prefer it closed and locked." His eyes burned into hers as if gauging her response and, knowing that she would disagree, he added, "for Jake's protection."

Then, he cocked one corner of his mouth upwards, flashing a dimple that hadn't come out of hiding until now.

"Oh." Chelsea stared at his dimple. OK. He apologized. And he was thinking of Jake. Maybe he could play nice after all.

Why, God? Why the marshals? Why not a brief visit from the sheriff's office? Or Child Protective Services? Anybody but the marshals.

"Renner and I usually operate on a first name basis. Do you mind if we call you Chelsea?"

Trey's mellow voice jolted her away from the plea, reminding her of manners. Hadn't her mother always taught her to filter words with kindness, to treat everyone with respect? How could she treat these men any differently just because of where they worked? "No, please do. I should have mentioned that earlier."

"That's OK. It's not every day two guys show up on your doorstep toting badges and guns." Trey grinned, allowing her a chance to see the dimple on the other side of his face. "But, rest assured, we carry good insurance."

Chelsea smiled, her heart melting the tiniest bit. OK, so he was a little funny, too. "That's good to know. Insurance, as in the guns you carry?"

"What else?"

"Well, I hope we don't have to utilize the insurance, if you know what I mean." She cast a knowing glance in his direction.

He nodded. "We're hoping for a quiet stay as well."

Trey turned to look at Jake, who was paying more attention to his meatballs than the conversation.

"We should probably go over a couple things," Trey continued. "Please forgive me for taking the liberty of shutting the window. I know it's wonderfully cool outside for summer, but for safety's sake, all of ours, we need to keep the windows closed and locked. At dusk, we'll need to draw the blinds. And please, don't go outside without me."

"What?" Chelsea raised eyebrows and tilted her head sideways, glancing quickly at Jake before narrowing eyes at Trey. What just happened here? "What does this have to do with me? It's Jake you need to worry about. Jake's your star witness. Not me. I'm nobody in your scheme of things."

Trey grimaced, and Chelsea saw the pleading look he sent his partner's way. Just in time for Renner to tuck his head downward, quickly spearing spaghetti with his fork.

"Didn't Hamilton tell you?"

"Didn't Hamilton tell me what?" Chelsea waited, the brownies she'd ingested earlier settling like boulders in her stomach.

"Jake's being moved to a safe house. I've been given orders to stay here and protect you for a few days."

3

"What?" Her fork landed with a thump on the plate. Did he just say what she thought he said? Protect her?

"It's only for a few days."

"A *few* days?" She stared at Trey, sensing the unyielding line of his jaws, the straightness of his shoulders, and knew this man expected cooperation. Her cooperation. She tried to concentrate on his words, but her brain had hit the OFF switch. "Like...how many days?"

"Just until we make sure that nobody followed Jake here. That Carp—Jake's father doesn't have anybody out looking for him." Trey looked from Renner to Jake, probably searching for assistance, but no one volunteered anything. He turned his attention back to her.

Chelsea grabbed a napkin to fan her flaming face. When her dad advised her to call the marshal's office for Jake, she envisioned them swooping in and taking Jake away. To safety. Away from her. Then, she could wash her hands of the entire situation. Including the marshals.

But, *stay* with her? *Protect* her? How was she supposed to get on with her life?

"What if Jake's father arranged for someone to track him down?" Trey asked, his face devoid of expression. "Would you like us just to leave you unprotected?"

Chelsea shot her gaze to Jake, noticing the twitching of his left eyelid and the way he pushed his dinner plate away.

Now the marshals had crossed the line. There was no way Chelsea would let these guys scare Jake into submission. She lifted her chin, squared her shoulders. She'd take them on. She threw her napkin on her plate and stood up.

"Do you mind if we continue this conversation privately?"

Trey glanced at Jake, apparently seeing the same things she did, because the creases around his eyes softened. "Sure. I'll help you with the dishes."

Did he really think she wanted him in the kitchen with her? Working side by side, elbow to elbow, at the sink? "Um, thanks, but that's all right. I can handle them myself."

"I insist." Trey stood up and reached for the dirty plates, stacking them into a pile.

He'd backed her into a brick wall. How could she get out of this?

"Well, since you two have the dishes covered, how about a game of pool, Jake?" Renner grinned and stood up, tossing an amused glance at Trey.

It was her turn to send pleading eyes towards Jake.

"Sure. Have you played before?" Jake, the traitor, didn't even look her way. He tossed his napkin on the table and stood up. He was probably just grateful dinner had ended, and the agents' attention hadn't landed on him.

"Oh, once or twice." They left the dining room,

their voices fading away, leaving Chelsea standing with her mouth hanging open. She closed it and gritted her teeth.

"You really don't have to help with the dishes. I can manage." Panic pricked at Chelsea's throat, and her voice came out strained. She loaded glasses and started towards the kitchen.

Trey followed with the plates. "I don't mind. The spaghetti was great, by the way. And I don't think I've ever tasted better garlic bread." He placed the dishes on the counter and lifted the faucet handle to fill the sink with hot water while he rolled up shirt sleeves. A light lemon fragrance filled the air when he squeezed dish soap into the flowing water.

Chelsea stood by the sink, uncertain what to do with someone else in control of her kitchen. Trey winked and handed Chelsea the dish towel. "Here. I'll load the dishwasher and wash the pans. You dry and put away since I don't know where anything goes in this gigantic kitchen."

Chelsea looked at the towel in his hands. The sooner she accepted his help, the faster she could escape. Away from those eyes that didn't miss a thing. Away from those biceps that bulged underneath his dress shirt. Away from the awareness that prickled through her body the longer she stood next to him.

Not happening! She would not allow herself to be attracted to a Deputy U.S. Marshal. "Thanks," she conceded and snatched the towel. "Are you always this bossy?"

"Mmm-hmm. Always. Just ask my sister."

Ask his sister? Like she would ever have the opportunity to do that. Or want the opportunity. With any luck, he'd be out of her hair by tomorrow night.

She removed her wedding ring and placed it in a dish beside the sink, blushing under his scrutiny.

"I don't remember Hamilton briefing us that you were married."

How was her marital status any of his business? One glance at his furrowed brows, the scowl masking his face, and she knew he'd make it his business. She took a deep breath, and then pushed it out even more slowly. She grabbed a clean pan from the dish drainer and attacked it with the towel. "I was. My husband was killed three years ago. Actually, by the same..."

The color drained from his face faster than the dishwater in the sink. "I'm sorry, Chelsea. We don't have to talk about it."

Thank you for that small favor. "So when is Renner doing the disappearing act with Jake?"

Warm eyes pleaded for her understanding.

She turned her head, avoiding his gaze and opened the cabinet for the pans, stowing one and shutting the door.

"Tonight."

Jake was leaving tonight? "Are you serious?"

"If it was up to me, Jake would already be tucked away in a safe house far from here."

OK. She was definitely changing the code on the alarm. "Why? Don't you think my place is safe? I've never had any problems. I don't even have any neighbors to complain about."

"It could be Fort Knox and it wouldn't matter."

Chelsea scoffed, whether from disbelief or nerves, she didn't know. "It really sounds like you're paranoid. Jake's father is in jail. Locked up tight. At least that's what Hamilton told me."

"Jake's father is locked up. At the moment."

"What's that supposed to mean?"

"It means he's a man with connections, including a lot of higher-up connections, like a judge. Who knows? What I know, from experience, is that he is a man who will stop at nothing to get what he wants."

If he was trying to scare her, it was working. "And what does he want right now?"

"Isn't that obvious?"

"Maybe to a marshal or a law enforcement officer. Not necessarily to a high school guidance counselor on summer break." One whose brain was seriously malfunctioning.

"Word travels fast. By now he knows that Jake has contacted us and is willing to testify. That means he'll stop at nothing to get to his son."

"To keep him from testifying?"

"Yes."

Chelsea hung the wet dish towel over the stove handle. "What do you think he would do?"

"Anything it takes. He has the money and the connections. He could try to snatch him or he could just put out a hit."

She froze with her hand on the refrigerator door. *Put out a hit?* "A hit? As in, have his own son killed?"

"Something like that."

Yep. Definitely paranoid. She didn't trust criminals as much as the next person but Carpocelli was in jail. Hello! Did Trey think Carpocelli had a "get out of jail free" card hiding in his orange jumpsuit?

"How well do you know Jake's father?" She couldn't mask the disbelief that laced her tone.

His head jerked up from fidgeting with his radio. His face darkened. How could he blame her for being suspicious?

"Well enough to know what he's capable of." Trey's lips formed a thin line and he clenched his hands.

Looked like thinking about Carpocelli had Trey wound pretty tight. Well, he could stand in line.

She had better things to do with her time than waste it on negative emotions or "what ifs." Wasn't she always telling the kids that? With her hand finally functioning, she opened the refrigerator door and pulled out the container of goat's milk. Chelsea retrieved the baby cereal from the cabinet and began mixing the formula together before putting it in the bottle. She stuck it in the microwave for thirty seconds.

"I need to go check on Molly."

"Who's Molly?"

She headed towards the mudroom, not bothering to enlighten him. He would figure it out soon enough. She turned around to see if he followed her, surprised that he still stood by the kitchen counter, staring at her. "Are you coming?"

"Yeah. Give me just one second." Trey snatched his portable radio from the table and requested perimeter checks.

"Clear. No activity since the last check."

"Clear here as well. All's quiet."

He nodded his head at the second response. "OK, thanks."

Chelsea slipped on tennis shoes by the back door and caught Trey's sneak peek at her.

He keyed his radio again. "Ms. Hammond and I will be walking outdoors for a few minutes."

"I didn't realize you and Renner brought reinforcements. How many agents are here?" Chelsea asked, alarm spreading inside her chest. Maybe Trey hadn't been exaggerating.

"Two outside. Two inside. Why?"

"Uh, I guess it's best to be prepared. It just seems a little excessive."

"Let's hope so. Let me tell Renner and Jake where we're going. I'll be right back." He disappeared into the game room. Chelsea peeked around the corner to watch.

"I'm going with Chelsea to check on Molly, whoever that is. I'll do the perimeter check while we're out."

Chelsea saw Renner lining up the eight ball and his raised eyebrows at Trey's words. "OK. We should be ready to move in a couple hours. After dark."

Trey glanced at his watch and nodded. "We'll be back in a few minutes."

"OK, I'll give you thirty before I send the troops after you."

Chelsea waited for Trey to catch up before she exited the mudroom with the warm bottle. Trey's hand rested lightly against her back as they walked outside. Each time he touched her, tingles traveled up her arms, like the little pin pricks of electricity they used in therapy at the chiropractor's office. She scurried forward, away from the tension his hand generated.

Crossing the yard, she headed towards the barn, the coolness of the evening breathing renewed life into her, the rhythm of the night sounds whispering peace to unsettled nerves. She shivered, but not from coolness.

She dared a glance at Trey's profile in the moonlight. His eyes scanned the distance, studying every detail. Little things like the stubborn set to his jaw, the stern position of his brows, and the permanent etchings around his eyes from squinting in the sun told her he worked too hard, played too little. If she was forced to spend time with him, maybe she could get him to relax a little, to kick back and enjoy his time here.

At least until tomorrow night. When she expected him to disappear.

How could the marshals expect anything to happen out here? With the gentle sway of the tree branches, the crickets chirping, and—she reached down to swat at a mosquito on her leg— um, cigarette smoke? She sniffed again. Must have been her imagination. Or maybe one of the outside agents smoked.

She started to enter through the open barn door but stopped when Trey touched her elbow. "Let me check the inside first."

Chelsea rolled her eyes. "Right now the only thing you'll find in there is Molly."

"And Molly is?"

"A baby deer who lost her mother a few days ago."

"Ahh. Molly, the one standing next to you earlier. I'll keep a lookout for her."

"She bunks in the first stall to the left." Chelsea whispered at his disappearing back.

A seed of doubt kicked Chelsea's heart rate higher. After stumbling into Jake last night, who was she to say that Trey wouldn't find anything? Or anybody.

He reappeared a minute later, and Chelsea released the breath she'd been holding. "All clear."

"I didn't doubt that." OK, maybe she had a little. "But thanks, though."

When was the last time somebody besides her

parents had worried about her? When was the last time she had *allowed* somebody to worry about her?

Chelsea snorted, leading the way to Molly's stall. Protecting her was Trey's job. Reading anything into it bordered on insanity. "So, I overheard Renner say they would be leaving in a couple of hours?"

"Yes." They stopped at the open stall door, and Trey entered first, bending down to hold out his hand for Molly to sniff like he would a dog. "Hey there, girl. Sorry to hear about your mama." With soft, gentle hands he stroked Molly's head and rubbed her ears.

She'd only experienced strong and confident Trey, the in-charge, won't-accept-no-for-an-answer Trey. Yet, in this simple act of stroking a motherless fawn, he'd also shown her that he was someone else. A man, vulnerable and tender, with a soft-hearted nature. One who didn't mind getting on his knees to care for an animal.

Here, in front of her, kneeled a man she might not mind getting to know. The first man in three years. Chelsea's jaw dropped. She caught herself before she allowed that thought to take root in her heart.

She *might* have considered it. If she had met him at church or through one of her friends. And, an even bigger *if* here—*if* he didn't have a law enforcement badge plastered across his chest.

She needed to convince him to leave tonight with Renner. She didn't need complications of the heart right now. Not with the shelter opening.

Her counselor instincts crept in. She had to make sure they'd take care of Jake before she could let him go. "So, what do you think of Jake?"

"He's better than I thought. I came with a preconceived opinion on what a mobster's son would be like. I'm glad I was proven wrong."

Ah. So the man was willing to admit his mistakes. *Drat.* Another positive quality.

She waited for Trey to rise to his feet before pulling the bottle from its hiding spot behind her back. Molly wobbled and stood, creeping closer, until she finally tugged on the bottle. That animal rehab company the vet had referred her to had better hurry up and get out here. Molly was becoming pretty attached. Or was it the other way around? "How so?"

"I expected him to be a spoiled rich kid, a brat. But he doesn't appear to be that way at all." Trey rubbed the fawn's neck while she ate.

"He isn't. At least not from what I can see, either."

"Tell me what your impression is."

"For one, he's scared."

"I would be too, if I were in his shoes. His dad is not somebody you want to tangle with."

The fawn finished the bottle, and Chelsea fluffed the straw around in the stall. "Good night, Molly. See you in the morning." She followed Trey out of the stall and latched the door. "Secondly, he misses his mother, just like this little sweetheart."

"Ahh."

Chelsea flipped the light switch off and closed the door. She shivered in the cool breeze after the warmth of the barn. She scooped out some dog food from a cooler by the door and filled the container for the resident ducks. And whatever other critters who chose to partake, like the squirrels and the crows. "What do you mean, 'ahh'?"

Trey led the way towards the tree line. "That explains the bond he's developed with you in such a short time."

"No, it doesn't. Haven't you noticed that I naturally exude charm?"

He'd been looking in the distance, but at her words, his head jerked towards her in time to see the teasing smile on her face. Mischief danced around his eyes. "I'm sorry. You're right. I don't think I'd be able to resist your charm or your cooking if I were fourteen. Maybe not even at thirty. But I'm older. Wiser."

She laughed, shaking her head. "If you had left off the 'older' and 'wiser' bit, I might have taken that as a compliment."

His eyes crinkled around the corners when he looked at her, and his lips curled into a killer smile. "I think I'd better let that one pass."

"Chicken," she teased.

They walked around the yard in silence. Trey scanned the distance, straining his ears to identify every sound. Chelsea stole glances at him, hoping he wouldn't notice.

She pushed an errant curl away from her face, so she could gauge his reaction from the corner of her eye. "So now that you know I'm safe, will you be leaving with Renner and Jake later tonight?"

"No."

No reaction at all? He didn't even raise his head. "Why not?"

"I told you."

Chelsea stopped walking, placing a pleading hand on Trey's arm. "But you've checked things out. You know it's safe here now. It'll be just me and Molly and Kalyn."

"And me."

She snatched her hand back. "But how can I possibly operate my shelter with you here?"

"You can't. We'll divert any arriving teens to the local social services agency until we trust that things are clear."

Chelsea stomped her foot. For a short while, he'd actually been likeable. Now, he was back to being impossible. "That will never work. How can I possibly expect to build up a good reputation as a shelter by sending the kids who come to me for help to social services?"

"With your natural charm, I'm sure you won't have any trouble on that end." He flashed his teeth. Was he joking or serious?

She narrowed her eyes. "OK, buddy, but just so you know, I've got lots of things planned for the next week and if you're sticking around, you'll just have to keep up."

He threw his head back, laughing. When he was finally able to contain himself, he smiled at her, amusement written all over his face. "We'll see."

"We'll see nothing." She stomped her foot. Again. Not that it did her any good the first time. "I'm not about to let you disrupt…"

Cigarette smoke wafted within her personal zone again, and she knew it wasn't Trey's aftershave scent now. "Do your agents smoke on duty?"

"No. Why?"

"Don't you smell that? The cigarette smoke?"

His nose wiggled. He frowned, practically grinding out the words. "Get back to the house. Tell Renner to secure Jake."

4

"I don't remember reading anywhere that entertainment was included in the price," Trey said.

Chelsea stopped singing but continued lightly strumming the guitar. She smiled and lifted sleepy eyes from her comfy spot nestled on the rug against the couch. Trey's shoulder rested against the door frame. His hands were tucked into the pockets of jeans that looked way too good on him. "I'm sorry. Did I wake you?"

He meandered into the great room, raking a hand through his mussed hair. "No. I hadn't fallen asleep yet. I think I'm just wound up from everything that happened tonight."

"But you didn't find anybody."

"No. We didn't. That doesn't mean somebody wasn't there." He settled down on the floor next to her, and those tingles traveled up and down her arms again at his nearness. Irritation prickles. That's what they were.

She cocked her head to one side, studying him. "So you expected to find somebody?"

"We always expect trouble." He rubbed the stubble on his cheeks, and she jerked her head the other way, the gesture feeling way too intimate.

"I'm glad Mr. Hamilton changed his mind and allowed Jake and Renner to stay a little longer."

No response. He wasn't happy about it.

She shrugged her shoulders. "It's always easier to say goodbye in the daylight."

The corner of his mouth lifted in a gentle curve, and one of those elusive dimples appeared briefly. "Why is that?"

"Haven't you noticed it? It's a natural phenomenon."

"You're a natural phenomenon, Chelsea Hammond." He chuckled, a warm, appealing sound before his face sobered. "Jake leaves when Hamilton says. You'll have to be prepared to say goodbye at a moment's notice. Daylight or otherwise."

She nodded. His words, soft and silky, tickled her ear and caused her insides to flutter. She needed to steer this conversation somewhere else. "So, if everybody is tucked in safely and all is well at Journey's End, why are you still wound up?"

He grinned at her. "It's in a deputy marshal's job description."

"Maybe you ought to change jobs." Peeking at him from under heavy lashes, she saw his eyes narrow, his jaw clench.

"Yeah. Maybe." He stretched those long legs out in front of him, crossing one over the other. "So what are you doing up?"

How could she answer that question honestly without giving away the truth? That she couldn't stop thinking about the way he'd approached Molly, the softness in his voice, the gentleness in his hands. He seemed to appreciate her humor. She'd go with that. "I have to show you how it's done."

"How what's done?" He lifted one eyebrow and quirked his lips sideways.

"If I had any other guests, I'd have to ask you to stop belting out songs in the shower. But since it's just the four of us, I guess I'll just have to put up with it."

It took a minute for her words to sink in, but when they did, he threw his head back and laughed. She smiled, glad to see that he could still laugh. It didn't seem like he did too much of that in his job.

He narrowed his eyes at her in a mock frown. "And what were you doing spying on me in the shower?"

"Spying?" She scoffed, warmth slowly creeping up her neck at his insinuation. "I wasn't spying on you."

"Then how do you know I belt out songs in the shower?"

"I could hear you downstairs all the way to the dining room. Your bathroom is the nearest to the stairwell."

"Ouch." He grinned and glanced at his watch. "I thought you said you were an early riser, but this is a little too early. It's got to be long past your bedtime."

"One a.m. is definitely past my bedtime. But I couldn't sleep. So here I am." Or rather, she didn't want to sleep.

"You don't look like you would have trouble sleeping. You can hardly keep your eyes open."

"I know. It's a case of my eyes want to close, but my brain doesn't want to stop working." Thoughts of what would happen to Jake after this painful episode in his life pulled her forward, but memories of Doug pushed her back. Memories so painful they had her poking the pillow in all different directions, finally persuading her to get up at midnight. Playing the guitar was balm to the wound, soothing her spirit. The only thing that helped her sleep. Like David playing the harp to Saul.

"Would you like some hot chocolate? I make a mean cup."

"Sure. That sounds nice. But I can make it." She placed the guitar against the couch and steadied herself to stand up.

He held up one hand to halt her progress while he used the other to push himself off the floor, as limber as a professional athlete. "No, please. Let me. You keep playing. It's beautiful. I'll be back in a minute."

Five minutes later Trey came back balancing two cups of hot chocolate loaded with whipped cream.

"Wow. This looks fabulous. Thanks, Trey." Setting the guitar down, she took the steaming mug from his hand. She took a slow sip and licked the heavy froth from her lips, savoring the rich chocolaty taste. "Mmm. You were right. This is delicious."

Trey stretched out to sit next to her on the floor, and she stole another glance at him. His sandy-colored hair, normally perfectly groomed, stood straight up, rumpled from sleep or from rubbing his hand through it. Thick eyebrows covered deep blue eyes, eyes the color of the ocean when sunny skies disappeared and dark clouds sauntered over.

Mystery lurked under those depths. Hidden secrets. What was he hiding?

He definitely wasn't hiding anything under that t-shirt. His arms sported biceps her brother would envy while his expansive shoulders strained against his shirt. Broad enough shoulders to lug around all the anxiety and tension inherent with his job.

Chelsea closed her eyes and sighed. So much for sleeping tonight. Not with that picture firmly settled in her head. She'd have to resort to cleaning now, rather than playing her guitar, something a little more physical. "What's your secret?"

"Huh?" He looked startled, like he really did have a secret, and almost spilled his hot chocolate.

"To the hot chocolate? Your secret ingredient to make it taste so good?"

"Oh. Just the normal stuff. Real milk with lots of chocolate and a little vanilla and sugar. Not the water and powder junk." He wrinkled his nose.

"Are you sure you're not holding out on me?" She smiled sweetly, knowing she was sending out mixed signals. What was he hiding?

"How did you name this place 'Journey's End'? And what made you decide to open a shelter for troubled teens?"

Ah, pretty smooth changing the subject. She lowered her gaze. So much for learning about the skeleton in his closet tonight. She shouldn't have pushed too hard. She blew on the hot chocolate and took another sip before answering. "That's a lot of questions for one in the morning."

He shrugged shoulders and met her gaze. "I seem to remember you saying that in this little corner of the world we have all the time we need."

She smiled and inwardly winced. *Drat.* The man had a good memory, using her words to come back and bite her. "It was a God thing."

He raised his eyebrows, his Adam's apple doing a little twitch. "A God thing?"

"Are you a Christian?"

"Yes. Although some may wonder about that the last few years. We haven't exactly been on speaking terms."

She smiled, gentle and without judgment,

knowing she'd been at that same point three years ago. "Then you know what I mean when I say it was a God thing. God led me here."

"How's that?"

"Two years after my husband died, I had no choice but to move away from Raleigh."

"Why? Not to sound insensitive, but other people have lost loved ones and not felt the need to move."

She flicked a curl behind her ear, taking a moment to think about it. "I know you're right. But for me, it didn't work that way. I had to leave. Not only was I born in Raleigh, but I grew up there, too. Doug and I had been friends since he moved into our neighborhood when I was ten years old. We got married right after we graduated high school. Half my life up until that point revolved around Doug."

Trey nodded for her to continue, listening with his head cocked slightly towards her. She could see her pain reflected from his eyes. Why was she telling him this? She hadn't even shared this with her best friend, Jamee.

She cleared her throat. "Doug had been dead for two years, but I still couldn't shake the memories. Everywhere I went. Everything I did. Just reading a newspaper article about a drug bust he helped work would reduce me to tears.

"If the days weren't long enough, the nights were intolerable. Every night I would come home from work and stare at his lumpy recliner. Or the remote." She paused and pain almost stole her voice. "Stupid remote. It's funny how little things like that affected me. That remote drove me insane. I finally just threw it in the garbage."

What she couldn't tell him was how she ate takeout meals standing in the kitchen so she didn't have to sit at the table by herself. Or that she hadn't slept an entire night in two years because of the bare spot in their king-sized bed and the aching in her heart.

An arm slid along the back of the couch, and she swallowed the heavy lump in her throat. A tear coursed down her cheek. Trey reached over and swiped it away with his thumb.

"Our friends stopped calling." She turned to look into Trey's eyes, his face close. She sniffled and swiped at her wet cheeks with the back of her hand. "I don't know if it was because I was single and suddenly they felt threatened or because I was the odd one out. Whatever it was, I found myself staying home more, closing myself off from everyone except my family. One day I woke up and realized I was wrapped in a cocoon so tight I felt the life being squeezed right out, one day at a time."

"I'm so sorry, Chelsea," Trey whispered. He reached for the tissue box on the end table and held it out to her.

"Thanks." She dabbed her nose with the tissue. He had to be tired of this story.

"Go on. Please."

She wrinkled her nose. "Surely there's better things for you to do than listen to my drama?"

He cocked his head to one side and frowned. "You can't leave me hanging like this. Please. I'd like to hear the rest."

She twisted the tissue. "Doug worked in undercover narcotics. When he was killed, the official line from the sheriff's office was that he wasn't on duty."

"In his line of work, he was always on duty."

"Yeah, well you know that, and I know that. But I'm sure you can picture the gossip that statement garnered." Her voice cracked from the torture of reliving the pain. "I felt the noose around my neck grow tighter every day, with all the stares and huddled whispers behind my back, at the school, even at church. The last straw was when my father saw it, too."

"Your father?" Surprise seeped into Trey's voice.

"Yes, my father. He'll be retiring this year after thirty years as a deputy in the sheriff's office."

"What did your father see?"

"One day at work I was walking out of my office when I overheard a couple teachers whispering behind me in the hallway. This wasn't the first time I'd overheard them, so I turned to confront them, but the words died on my lips. My father stood directly behind the pair. From his expression, I knew he'd heard it. Apparently, he came to surprise me for lunch." Chelsea exhaled loudly, a sob escaping her chest. "Imagine his surprise."

She didn't need to imagine. She could still picture the look of shock on his face, followed by rage. "At first he was angry at the teachers, their insensitivity, but then he was even angrier with himself for not noticing my pain until Mom mentioned it." Mom had pointed it out to him— the dark hollows under her eyes, the sagging of her chin, the perpetual slump of her shoulders.

"What did he do?"

"Dad marched me in to see the principal and helped me secure a personal leave until I decided what to do. I went home, packed my suitcase, loaded my guitar in the truck, and hopped in. Then I just drove. I drove until I stopped crying. Until I could no longer see any remnant of the man who had consumed so much of my life. I drove until I couldn't find myself on the map. But, that's not saying a lot." She sniffled and unsuccessfully tried to stifle a hiccup. "I'm not a good map-reader. I didn't find my way very far.

"God stopped me here. I told myself this was the end of the road. And when I saw the sign for Journey Creek, I knew God still had a plan for my life, even without Doug." That plan included comfort, consolation, peace, renewal. And now, maybe, forgiveness.

"And the teen shelter?"

His soft words could almost put her to sleep, they were so sweet and sincere. "The teen shelter has been a dream of mine since I was ten. Ever since Doug moved into our neighborhood."

"What did Doug have to do with your dream of opening a shelter?"

"Our neighbors, Henry and Stella, were really Doug's grandparents. Social Services brought Doug to them because his mom had walked out on him. Just walked out. Left him alone in their apartment for days." She shook her head. She couldn't tell him the rest. How Doug had to have his head shaved for lice after coming to live with Henry and Stella. How they gently scolded him for rummaging around in garbage cans and dumpsters, loathe to give up hunting for food and clothing. It took a couple years for him to break that habit.

She glanced at Trey, surprised to see he was still awake.

Relaxing against the couch, he had leaned towards her with his arm along the cushion. With gentle fingers, he brushed a stray curl away from her eyes. She blinked. There it was, those tingles running up and down her arms again.

She blushed. What was she doing here? She had just told a perfect stranger her life story. What did he care? She glanced at her watch and gasped. Two o'clock. Time to wrap it up or she wouldn't be up for breakfast in a few hours. Why had she gone on so? "So you see. It was a God thing."

Trey lifted his mug of hot chocolate and held it out to hers. "To a celebration of your new life as the caregiver for abandoned and neglected teens who so desperately need attention. I know your shelter will be a success. Not because of that natural charm you so humbly talk about, but because of who you are, inside."

They clinked mugs. Chelsea smiled through her tears. Tears of peace. Tears finally without pain.

5

Traipsing downstairs to the sounds of Chelsea's sweet music after midnight was just asking for trouble. A stunt like that could get him taken off the case. Maybe he should just call Hamilton. Beat him to the punch.

Except Trey didn't want to. For the first time in three years, he felt alive. Like sunshine had sailed back into his life. Or that the air he breathed was no longer stagnant, but filled with jasmine. Chelsea's scent.

Trey washed the dishes in the sink with more force than necessary, almost breaking a coffee mug. He dried them with a little more care and then stowed them in the cabinets where they belonged.

He hung up the dish towel and glanced at his watch. Two thirty a.m.

Another half hour.

He found where Chelsea kept the coffee and started a fresh pot.

Hamilton had made it clear on the phone last night that he wanted Jake pulled out at three a.m. if the remainder of the night was uneventful. It had been.

If he didn't count his hot chocolate sipping encounter with Chelsea.

OK. Uneventful as far as Hamilton was concerned.

He couldn't say the same for himself.

He'd rather take on a dozen Carpocellis than

spend any more time alone with Chelsea. Give him a crime to solve, a criminal, a gun, and he knew what to do. He'd come up with a plan and see that the plan was carried out. Calmly. Efficiently. No second-guessing himself.

Give him a hundred-and-forty-pound feisty female, force him to escort her in the moonlight where the stars magnified her shimmering green eyes and formed a halo out of her auburn tresses, and then throw a guitar-strumming-hot-chocolate-drinking session in. What did he do?

Panic, that's what. He was losing complete control of his senses.

He stuffed an antacid in his mouth while he waited for the coffee to brew.

Hands down. He'd rather deal with Carpocelli.

What he couldn't deal with was knowing that the pain reflected in Chelsea's gaze was caused by him. If he could take the suffering from her and shoulder it himself, he would.

No, he couldn't tell her about Doug. He didn't want to hurt her any more than he already had. The best thing he could do for Chelsea was to force the issue of a speedy trial for Carpocelli, get Jake out of here and leave, so she could heal.

The sooner, the better. For his own peace of mind. And hers.

Carpocelli's freedom was at stake here. Years of undercover work, not only his, but others as well. He couldn't risk anything happening to the kid. Carpocelli had to stay locked up. Locked up tight, as in, throw away the key. He had to keep focus.

That meant no more moonlit walks with Chelsea. No more middle-of-the-night chats.

If he could help it.

He checked his watch. Two forty-five. Time to wake Renner and Jake. They had to move.

He grabbed two mugs from the cabinet and poured coffee into both, adding one packet of sweetener in his. Renner preferred his coffee black. He didn't know what the kid would want.

He trudged up the stairwell carrying both mugs and met Renner closing the door to his room, already dressed, his overnight bag sitting on the carpet in the hall. Trey handed him a mug.

"Thanks." Renner took a long slug of his coffee and knocked on Jake's door. Opening the door, he called, "Jake, time to get up. Let's get going."

Incoherent mumbling emanated from the bedroom. "Heavy sleeper," Trey said.

Renner's grin split the dark stubble covering his face, as he swung the door back to allow Jake privacy to dress. "Probably no worse than I was at fourteen."

"You mean no worse than you are now?" Trey countered, knowing Renner could sleep through a fire alarm.

"Hey, I'm up, aren't I?"

Chelsea's door creaked open and a bleary gaze appeared around the frame. She honed in on Renner's suitcase in the hall; her lips parted in an "oh." "Are you guys leaving *now*?"

"Yeah." Trey nodded once, his pulse accelerating at her husky voice. Her door closed and a minute later she reappeared in the hallway wearing the shorts and t-shirt she had on just an hour earlier.

"Is Jake up?"

Renner peeked in the room. "Need some help there, buddy?" He walked into the bedroom, leaving the door open.

"How long will they be traveling?" Chelsea asked, twisting a curl around her finger.

"They're not going too far, Chelsea. Why?" The chief thought it best for them to stay closer to Charlotte, away from Raleigh. Too close to Chelsea, in his opinion.

"I'll fix them something to take while you guys wait for Jake to load that gargantuan backpack of his."

Renner returned to the hallway and heard her comment. "Gargantuan doesn't come close. I had to help him hoist that thing on his back. And we'll take more of those brownies, if you have some leftover. Trey made coffee already." He lifted his mug for her to see.

"Then I'll make you a fresh to-go cup and meet you guys downstairs."

Trey watched her walk down the stairs and turned to meet Renner's smirk. "I wondered who would finally catch your interest. And when. It's funny, though. I don't think I ever expected it to be Hammond's widow. Not in a million years."

Trey sipped his coffee and glared at his partner over the rim of his mug. "Who said I was interested?"

Renner raised his eyebrows. "Are you going to tell me you're not?"

"Not what?" Jake stepped out of his room, a heavy book bag draped over one shoulder.

"Not tired, even though I've been up all night." A change of subject was in order. Anything to get Renner and Jake going. Away from the danger Jake directed to Chelsea. Away from the discussion Renner wanted to continue, judging by the snickering he wasn't even trying to restrain. "Chelsea's packing you guys something to take with you, Jake. Are you hungry? Do you want something to drink?"

"Yeah."

Trey pointed his arm towards the stairwell. "Let's go. You ready?"

"Not really. When we get to where you're taking me, can Chelsea come see me?"

"We'll have to work on that, buddy. I don't know." Trey followed Jake and Renner down the stairs. He felt sorry for the kid. Arriving in a strange place with no friends or family to trust, he attached to someone who made him feel safe. And now the marshals come in to whisk him away. Tough break. Trey knew he'd have to touch base with Hamilton on Chelsea visiting. Or tagging along.

Chelsea handed Renner a fresh coffee and a heavy basket. "Muffins, brownies, fruit to munch on."

"Thanks."

"You're welcome." Chelsea turned towards Jake and cleared her throat. "Come here, sweetie. Give me a hug."

Trey's throat clogged at the picture Chelsea made, hugging a gangling teenager at least a foot taller than she was, tears welling in her eyes. "This isn't goodbye because I'll see you again."

"I already asked Trey. He said they'd work on it."

Trey would do anything for that flash of gratitude Chelsea sent his way. Including calling Hamilton and suffering through his abuse.

"You're doing the right thing by testifying; you just keep remembering that." Chelsea nudged Jake backwards so she could look into his face. "And if these guys don't take good care of you, you have my number." Chelsea pressed a piece of paper into Jake's hand.

Trey pretended not to see that.

Renner looked the other way.

Maybe Trey would keep his partner after all. "Renner and Jake will be best buds before this is over with. You'll see. OK, let's load 'em up."

❧

Chelsea followed Jake to the front door, her stomach clenching with fear. It was too soon. Something didn't feel right. Why hadn't they warned her they were taking him? Was that what Trey tried to tell her earlier? To be prepared for Jake to leave at any time? He was probably trying to break it to her gently. But it felt like a boulder dropped on her head with no warning.

"Are you sure you don't want me to go with you?"

"You've got your big gig on Sunday." Jake reminded her.

"But you know if you need me to I would…"

"I'll be all right, Chelsea. Renner will take good care of me. Not quite as good as you do, though." He grinned, gave her a one-armed hug and followed Renner out the front door, his shoulders drooping from the weight of the backpack.

Her head sagged against the front door while she watched Jake hop in the backseat next to Renner. A marshal she didn't recognize sat in the driver's seat. Trey said a few words to them and closed the door.

Jake's voice said one thing, but Chelsea's heart told her something different. Could she let Jake go by himself? Not really by himself, she amended, he was heading to the safe house with Renner. And Trey eventually, if she convinced him she could fend for herself. They would take good care of Jake...

Wouldn't they? Would Hamilton let her see Jake at the safe house? Could she trust the marshals, period?

"Hey. Are you OK?"

Uh, no.

The I-feel-sorry-for-her look in his eyes just about caused her to unravel. What was going on? She'd felt so content the last few days, so at peace with life. Now she felt as if her heart was being ripped apart again.

She took a deep cleansing breath, and then opened her eyes to find Trey lounging against the wall next to her, his hand inches from her hair. She sucked in a breath at his closeness. "I'm OK." Hating that her voice came out wobbly, she pulled the wedding ring off and slid it back on. Off. On. *Stop it!*

"I'm sorry I couldn't give you more warning about this, Chelsea."

The car pulled away and headed down the long driveway towards the road, taking Jake away from her. Poor Jake. His heart bleeding over the loss of his mother, and now they were hauling him away to who knows where.

She should have gone with him for support. He was all alone in the world. And he was trying to make good choices, tough choices.

She sighed and pushed away from the door. She'd just have to make it up to Jake.

~~∽∽~~

Trey tugged the comforter over his head, trying to buy a couple more hours of sleep. As if he could, with sunlight bursting through the curtains of his bedroom window and…

What was that noise? That loud squawking? He could handle the hundreds of chirping birds, but that squawking was getting annoying.

Trey pushed the comforter back far enough to focus his eyeballs on the alarm clock. It couldn't be eight o'clock already, could it?

His nose twitched when he caught a whiff of strong coffee brewing. Chelsea must be up.

He yanked the thick comforter off and stretched his legs over the side of the bed. He smiled, thinking of Chelsea's comments about having lots of things to do this week. Time to see what was on her agenda. Sleeping until eight wouldn't cut it, if she was up and ready to go.

He pulled the curtains back from the window and squinted at the bright sunshine. Majestic pine trees and dazzling maple trees towered over the yard, teeming with blue birds, cardinals and crows. Dew glistened on the grass under the blue canopy sky, not a cloud in sight. Two mature mallards and their five babies paced around the food dish Chelsea had filled by the barn door the night before. There they were—the quacking culprits.

Why did the day seem more vibrant, more alive, out in the country? He could wake to the same blue sky in Raleigh, but it didn't seem to hold near the appeal as this farmhouse.

Maybe because he didn't hear the traffic snarling down the highway or obnoxious car horns beeping by people competing to get to their jobs before traffic worsened. Didn't they know it was just a vicious cycle?

Yeah, he could live with this slower pace, this radiant energy. *No*, he groaned, *he couldn't*. He was here to do a job, his job, and he shouldn't forget that. That's all this was. That's all it could be. A job.

He cast a quick glance over the yard and beyond the barn, but all he noticed were the trees. Tons of trees. If Carpocelli's man was out there, he'd be right on top of them before they knew he was here.

Trey shook his head and lowered the curtain. He'd better stop musing and get a move on or he would miss breakfast. Chelsea was probably stomping that foot of hers. Nah, knowing her, she probably hadn't waited on him. He made his way into the bathroom, erasing the smile that snuck up.

He couldn't let Chelsea's gentle manner and her sweet spirit chip away at the fortress he had erected around his heart. Because then he'd be forced to tell her the truth.

He inspected his shaving job, satisfied he hadn't caused any blood loss, and walked back into the bedroom.

His radio squealed, and he bent over to pick it up from the charger on the nightstand. "Colten here."

"Sir, we have a car headed in our direction. Looks like an older style Chevy Malibu. How do you want me to handle it?"

Good. Jenkins was back on duty. Trey trusted him more than Reynolds. "Stop it. I believe it's probably Kalyn returning, but check it out and call me back."

"Ten-Four. I'll report back shortly."

Trey pulled on jeans and t-shirt, thankful that he showered last night, and tucked his gun in the back of his pants. If it wasn't Kalyn, who would be visiting Chelsea so early?

They'd find out. He grabbed the radio and headed downstairs.

The aroma wafting from the kitchen stopped him on the stairs. Fresh coffee, bacon and eggs? If the sun streaming through his window or the squawking ducks hadn't woken him earlier, this would have. His stomach growled.

"Mmm. This smells absolutely wonderful."

Chelsea jumped and pieces of jellied toast scattered all over the floor. "Ah! Don't you think you should warn me when you're around? You could have had jelly all over that nice... "

Her gaze skimmed his t-shirt, and her face turned red. "Never mind." She bent down and picked up the toast.

"Here, let me get this for you." He winked at her wide gaze before tearing off some paper towels. After running water over them, he bent down to finish cleaning up the sticky mess.

His radio sounded again, and he grabbed it while he continued wiping the floor. "Colten here."

"Sir, you were right. It's Kalyn Sommers. Pregnant. Seventeen according to her ID. Says she's the housekeeper for the shelter."

Pregnant? Trey looked up at Chelsea. She was stirring something on the stove, but turned to face him when the radio blared. "Kalyn is pregnant?"

Chelsea nodded.

"Kalyn is one of your teens?"

"Kalyn is a teen, and yes, she's pregnant, but she's not here as a resident of the shelter, if that's what you're asking." She put the toast on the plate before continuing, waving the jelly knife in the air. "Kalyn wouldn't stay here without paying her way. So she is my housekeeper; but more than that, she's my friend."

He grimaced, knowing what was coming next. She

wasn't going to like it, not one bit, but he had to ask. Kalyn being pregnant added a whole different dimension to their situation. "Do you think she might be able to find another place to stay for the next few days?"

Chelsea slapped the knife on the counter and faced him, hands on her shapely hips, deep green eyes flashing like wild waters swirled by hurricane winds. "No."

"Why not?"

"She has nowhere else to go. Her parents kicked her out when they found out she was pregnant. I will not ask her to leave."

Trey nodded, careful to conceal the lopsided grin that suddenly threatened to invade his face. If she could, Chelsea would probably take in every homeless teen in a fifty-state radius. Not to mention homeless animals of every variety. "OK. We'll make do."

"What do you mean 'we'll make do?' When will you leave and let me get on with running my shelter?"

"When Hamilton gives the order. A couple more days. At least." A playful thought struck him, and he gave in to the desire to have some fun with it. He tilted his head sideways and appeared thoughtful. "But, it could end up being a couple weeks."

"A couple of weeks! You can't possibly mean that. Get Hamilton on the phone for me."

Now waving a wooden spoon in the air, Chelsea looked ready to riot. The last thing Trey needed was for her to call Hamilton and get him riled up. Maybe he'd gone a little too far for fun.

Too much was at stake. Like keeping Carpocelli out of circulation. For good.

Not to mention his job. Hamilton would have his

hide. He could hear his thunderous voice already. *I told you, Colten, if you wanted a job to come back to, you'd better protect that widow with everything you've got.*

OK. He'd let her get by with her threats. At least for now. He keyed his radio. "We verified Kalyn Sommers lives here. Go ahead and let her by."

Trey turned to face Chelsea and spoke softly. He wanted her to understand his position. "Chelsea, I'll do everything in my power to protect the both of you, I promise, but I am only one person and my job is to protect you. I would feel so much better if Kalyn could stay with some friends. Even if it's just for a few nights."

He knew she considered what he was asking. "She's been through so much, Trey. She knows the risks of living in a shelter where troubled teens can come and go. I can't ask her to uproot again because of a slim chance Jake's father sent someone out to find him."

Trey raked a hand through his hair and heaved a loud sigh. Frustration rippled through his nerves.

"But I will do this for you."

She was willing to compromise? He raised his eyebrows.

"I will discuss this situation with Kalyn and how you feel about it. I will offer her options, such as staying with my friend, Jamee, or staying here. We'll let her make the choice."

Relief exploded in his chest.

"Does that help?"

"Tremendously." He knew Kalyn would make the right choice. She would want to protect her baby, right? "Thank you, Chelsea."

6

"How did you get your scar?" Chelsea still couldn't believe that Trey had agreed to sit outdoors this morning. Actually, she hadn't given him a choice. After Trey helped feed Molly and the ducks, Chelsea made more coffee and grabbed her Bible, heading for the outdoor oasis on the back deck, leaving him sitting alone at the kitchen table. Of course, he'd followed and demanded an explanation. She calmly explained that this was her routine and if he was sticking around, he'd better adjust. Chelsea compromised by pulling a couple large palms to block where they sat.

Trey took a long sip of coffee before setting the mug on the table. "Shrapnel wound." His fingers rubbed the scar along his jaw line. "From when I served in the Marines."

Surprise lodged in Chelsea's throat. "You served in the Marines? For how long?"

"Four years."

"Why did you choose to leave after four years? You didn't want to make it a career?"

His eyebrows furrowed, and she winced. *A little too personal.*

"Sorry. Blame it on my job as a school counselor. I've been trained to ask questions. Maybe too many, right?" She reached for her wedding band, pulled it to the tip of her finger, and slipped it back on.

He cleared his throat, and his eyes took on a glazed look, staring off in the distance. "That's OK. I stayed in long enough to see six buddies die over three tours of duty in four years. Long enough to know I didn't want to do that for sixteen more. I got out when a friend helped me land a spot with the marshals."

Chelsea lowered her head, allowing him space, time. How could one person handle all that pain? She'd only lost one buddy, her best friend, and could hardly cope.

With a slight shake of his head, he seemed to snap back into the present.

"And you've been a marshal ever since?"

"Yeah, thirteen years. It's a good living. Not much time for anything else, though."

Obviously not much time for fun. Or for a wife and family. "I can see that. You must travel a lot."

"Actually, that's all I've ever known in my adult life. In the Marines and with the marshals. In the beginning, it was fun traveling to all sorts of exotic locations. Africa, Spain, Portugal, Jordan, Kuwait. I've been to places most people never get a chance to visit. Truly amazing."

A big hairy spider crawled across the porch floor in front of her legs. She froze, unable to move, talk, even breathe. Trey flicked it off the porch with his shoe.

"Better?"

"Yeah." She released a nervous giggle. "Sorry. I spent a week in the hospital after a spider bit me when I was twelve. Obviously, it left lasting memories. And now?"

"Now?" He looked at her with one eyebrow raised.

"You said in the beginning it was fun. What about now?"

He scowled. "Now, I guess I'm getting a little too old to travel so much. The excitement has worn off. I'd rather spend more time at home and less away." His lips curved in a lazy grin. "But then I wouldn't have seen your beautiful place. Or met you."

"You better watch it. I might think you're flirting, and I know you don't want to give me that impression."

He laughed, a hearty sound that made warmth spread up her neck. That grin of his was getting to her. His sweet words reached down, and a warm feeling blanketed her stomach, like the hot chocolate from last night. For being such a tough guy with an even tougher job, she was finding hidden layers to Trey Colten. A gentle man. A man with feelings. A man who stirred her emotions.

She knew his gaze constantly roamed, searching for danger. The only real threat right now came from those tingles that crept up and down her arms when she was close to Trey.

"Will you be leaving today?"

"Trying to get rid of me again?"

"Yes."

He grinned and crossed his legs. "Not so fast. Just when I thought you were beginning to enjoy my company."

She rolled her eyes. Maybe she should try his own scare tactic on him. "We're having a cookout here tomorrow afternoon."

His eyebrows elevated. "Oh?"

"Mmm-hmm. With a bunch of teenagers." Wouldn't that scare most men off?

"Outside?" Popping one of his ever-present antacids in his mouth, he narrowed his eyes.

"I'm not sure how many cook*outs* you've been to indoors, but I can't say that I've ever been to any. I think by definition they are outdoors." She grinned. She could taste the victory, see the white flag waving. He'd be out of her hair by tonight at the latest.

The poor guy would have real problems eating out back tomorrow afternoon. Throw twenty or more teenagers into the mix...the man might eat an entire roll of antacids. Chelsea refused to put her life on hold because Jake's father, the one behind bars, *might* have sent someone to see if Jake was at her place. Whoever he sent would find that Jake wasn't here anymore.

If Trey had a problem with that, he could leave, right?

So why did she feel the tiniest bit of guilt tugging at her heart? "Jake's not here anymore, Trey. He's tucked away in a safe house. We'll be fine. Just like we are now," Chelsea said, placing a gentle hand on his arm.

"Yeah, but—" Trey scrunched his eyebrows together, obviously trying to come up with an excuse not to eat outside.

She mimicked his scrunched eyebrows, but kept the smile to let him know she was jesting. Mostly. "Hey, buddy. Didn't I warn that if you were sticking around, we were going to be busy? We're heading to the grocery store in a few minutes, we've got to get ready for the cookout tomorrow afternoon, I need to see for myself that Jake's—"

"OK."

OK? Her coffee cup rattled on the table top where she dropped it. Had he just given in? So easily? "OK, what?"

"OK. I got it. We'll be hosting a cookout tomorrow afternoon with twenty odd teenagers."

He might have gotten it, but he didn't look happy about it. "That's kind of an oxymoron, don't you think? Odd teenagers? Have you ever known a teenager you didn't feel was odd?"

"I think you're trying to trap me here. I refuse to take the bait."

She laughed and crooked her index finger, scoring one for him.

His dark eyes twinkled. "Did I pass?"

"Pass what?"

"This test that you seem to be grading me on."

She grinned. He'd caught on to her. "Maybe. You're actually sitting outside, smiling. You seem to be enjoying yourself."

"I am. Unlike this case, usually I'm sitting in some remote safe house guarding some hardened criminal who's decided to turn state's evidence just so he doesn't have to put in any jail time. I much prefer your company and this beautiful house."

"Thank you. I think." Chelsea rolled her eyes. "And when you put it like that, I think I would agree with you."

Trey smiled, lazily tilting his head to the side, twinkles shimmering from his eyes. "Wonders will never cease."

She stopped her grin and wrinkled her nose at him. "What about Kalyn?"

His smile faded. He shook his head, furrowed his brows. "What about Kalyn?"

Kalyn's decision to stay with them frustrated Trey. With all his worries about Carpocelli's henchmen, she couldn't blame him. On the other hand, she couldn't offer Kalyn a place to stay and then jerk it away from her. Kind of like what happened with Jake. It just wasn't fair. "What should she do while we're at the grocery store?"

He appeared deep in thought. "Do you know what her plans are for today?"

"No, but, today's Saturday. She may already have plans with her boyfriend."

Trey nodded. "Jenkins will still be here, but it would definitely make me feel better if she were away from the property while we're not here. I can't be two places at one time."

"I'll find out when we go back inside." She picked up her Bible. This was her reading spot, her private time with God. With Trey here, she'd have to share it for a few days.

"I'm ready." Trey guzzled the last of the coffee. He stood up and peered around the plants. "Let's go." He grabbed her hand, ushering her to the back door, keeping her next to the house while he used his body as a shield.

Wasn't he taking this a bit far? "Trey, I think I can find my way—"

Trey reached for the door handle.

She heard a buzzing noise and stepped aside.

"What…?" Trey muttered.

Hands grasped her shoulders and shoved her towards the wall. She closed her eyes, bracing for the impact.

7

"It's a hummingbird! They do this when one of their feeders goes empty. It takes them a few minutes to realize the other feeder still has food in it." Chelsea's voice was muffled by his shirtfront.

Trey relaxed. Marginally. His heart was still racing. "A hummingbird? I was just attacked by a hummingbird." His tone was flat. His hands were gripping Chelsea's shoulders, flattening her against the house, and he was using his body as protection. He made an effort to appear calm.

The guys would never let him live this down. He counted his blessings that Renner had left already and that none of the other agents were in the immediate vicinity. Maybe he could keep it under wraps.

Chelsea's breath fanned his neck in cool wisps. Jasmine drifted around his head. He stepped back, releasing his hold, away from her nearness, her sweetness.

She laughed, humor lighting up her face. She was too close for his peace of mind. He took another step backwards.

"If you stick around, I won't need to fill up my feeder to enjoy the hummingbirds."

"Very funny."

Chelsea giggled and went in search of Kalyn and her purse.

Trey walked the length of the deck, making sure the hummingbird hadn't been hurt by the quick sideswipe of his arm. He glanced over the rail, breathing a sigh of relief when he didn't see the tiny critter. No more wounded or homeless animals for Chelsea to rescue. He alerted Jenkins to their plans.

Chelsea opened the door and stepped outside with her purse and a shopping list. "Kalyn is leaving for her boyfriend's house in about five minutes. His parents invited her to a family reunion so she won't be back until long after we return."

"Good." He followed her to an older pickup. She reached for the driver's side door. He hesitated. Dare he ask?

She opened the door and turned to look at him with raised brows. "Did you forget something?"

"Would you mind if I drove?"

She smiled and tossed him the keys before heading around to the passenger door. "Control issues?"

Thank you! He snatched the keys from the air and followed her. He pulled antacids out of his pocket and popped one in his mouth before she saw him. Should he tell her that he suffered from nausea any time he sat in the passenger seat of a moving vehicle? Not a chance. "Let's just say I'll feel a lot more comfortable in the driver's seat."

"Yeah. Yeah. You men are all alike. You have to be in control. Driver's seat, remote control for the TV, whatever."

He opened the passenger door for her and caught her snicker. He held out his hand to help her up. Her face reddened, and she stared at his hand before looking up at him with wide eyes.

He cleared his throat. "It's a hike up there."

She took hold of his hand. "Thanks."

He made his way around to the driver's side and quickly cranked the engine, making sure the air conditioning vents were adjusted to blow air in both directions. "So, where are we heading?"

"Let's go into town. Grocery store first."

"Gotcha."

Trey followed her directions into Journey Creek and pulled into a parking spot at the grocery store. He opened the door for her and held out his palm.

"Thanks, Trey." She stepped down and gave a gentle tug for him to release her hand.

He didn't let go, holding steady when she looked at him with questions in her eyes. "Chelsea. Promise me you won't leave my side."

She wrinkled her nose. "I can't say that I've ever needed help grocery shopping before. But hey, if you're willing to push the cart and unload the groceries, I'll stick to you like gum on hot pavement."

He grinned and shook her hand before releasing it. "Done. Like gum on hot pavement."

He grabbed a shopping cart and tested the wheels. He hated getting one with wheels that wouldn't turn. He found the ideal cart on the second try and turned to find her stifling a grin.

"What?"

"Control issues again?" she asked, eyebrows raised. Humor lined her lips.

"Not even. Who wants to drive a cart with wheels that won't turn?"

She giggled. "Race car driver wannabe."

"Where are we headed first?"

"Let's see." Chelsea unfolded her shopping list

and scanned it. "Fruits and veggies."

He pushed the cart towards the produce section.

She followed him, still scanning the list. "I hope you're not one of those hurry-up-and-get-out shoppers. We're going to be here for awhile."

Chelsea paused at the watermelons. She picked one up and tapped it before putting it in the cart and moving on to the cantaloupes. Trey ambled along beside her, using the time to study the shoppers nearby. A woman with a sleeping baby in an infant carrier in the upper portion of the cart hurried to finish her grocery shopping. A woman behind them scolded two sulking pre-teens. Another woman made goofy eyes at a fussy toddler. An older man, toting a reusable bag, meandered around, looking lost. And the produce manager straightened the bell peppers.

His gaze skidded to a stop at the man who ducked in the front door, glancing first left and then right, missing Trey and Chelsea in his line of vision. Thirty-ish, suit, no cart, no basket. Trey kept his attention plastered on him. The guy averted his face and entered the store through the check-out counters. Practically running. Definitely out of place. Worth investigating.

Trey pushed the cart against the watermelon bin and grabbed Chelsea's hand. "Let's go check something out."

She gasped, turning to gaze at him with wide eyes. With a nod she threw the cantaloupe back into the bin and stayed close to his side.

He tugged her hand, pulling her closer. Close enough that he could no longer smell the fresh fruit or the lingering odor of seafood from the back of the store. He could only smell Chelsea. Jasmine, summer, sweetness.

She was getting to him. He tamped down feelings, pushed the jasmine further back to the deep recesses of his brain. If he didn't stay focused on doing his job, Chelsea could get hurt.

Trey glanced down the wine aisle in case the guy had retraced his steps. Nobody. They raced past the canned veggies and fruits. Only women. They continued jogging past pastas and baked goods. Just as they were nearing the frozen food section a little old lady pulled out of the aisle without looking, slamming her cart into his leg.

He reached down to rub the sudden pain gripping his leg, keeping one hand wrapped around Chelsea's. The lady backed her cart away from them, horror widening her eyes.

"Oh, son. I'm so sorry. Have I hurt you?"

So much for focusing. He glanced towards the checkout counter in time to see the man scurrying out the front door. No bags. No purchases. Who was he? Why had he been in the store? Trey would fire up his laptop when he got back to Chelsea's, see if he could find this guy's mug on any databases.

"No, ma'am. I'm OK. We shouldn't have been rushing through the store like that. Sorry to have bothered you."

"That's quite all right, young man. Although I have to say, I just can't understand why young people are in such a hurry nowadays." She pushed her cart around the corner, and Trey could still hear her mumbling. "Computers, cell phones, i-whatevers. Something always keeping people mighty busy..."

He gripped Chelsea's elbow, steering her away from the lady, a small smile gripping his lips. "She moves pretty fast for someone her age. You OK?"

She smiled back, taking a deep breath and fanning her red face with her shopping list. "Yeah. Just a little shook up. Who or what were we looking for?"

"A man that's long gone now."

Fear clouded her eyes. He could have kicked himself for frightening her unnecessarily. "Somebody came after us?"

"Not that I know of. I just wanted to check him out. I'm sorry for the wild goose chase." He grabbed her hand again and smiled. "Let's get back to this marathon shopping excursion of yours."

They walked back to the produce section and retrieved their cart. Trey waited until Chelsea busied herself with shopping again before pulling out his cell phone. He dialed Jenkins's number and alerted him to what had happened. Just to be on the safe side.

Had trouble come knocking already? Or was this some random guy who couldn't find what he wanted in the store?

ॐ∽

Something about those eyes. Chelsea couldn't quite figure who they reminded her of.

Chelsea stared at Trey from the passenger seat of her truck. He had a rugged face marked with scars to prove his desire for justice and freedom; strong, dependable shoulders that constantly hauled around the worries inherent with his job; and killer dimples, dimples she'd witnessed come out of hiding a few times, but not nearly enough.

But those eyes. They reminded her of someone. Who? It would come to her eventually. She needed to focus her energy and thoughts on the cookout tomorrow.

Chelsea shook her head to clear her thoughts and opened the center console. She pulled out an energy bar and held it up. "Want one?"

Trey glanced at the bar and shook his head before glancing back out the front window. "No, thanks."

She unwrapped it and took a bite. "Sorry, but I needed to eat something."

"And you just happened to carry energy bars in your truck?"

She nodded, chewing, and then swallowed. "I have to. I've been having some low sugar levels here recently. The doctor hasn't quite figured out what the issue is yet."

Trey's head jerked in her direction. "What kind of problems are you experiencing?"

"I get light-headed, almost like I want to faint."

Trey flipped the blinker on and turned down the road leading to her place. He hit the brakes and leaned forward in his seat, peering out the windshield. "Whoa. What's this?"

Chelsea looked at him before focusing on the puppy, a yellow lab with drooping tail, standing motionless in the middle of the road, scrunching up a mangled leg. The pup's large mournful eyes glimmered with pain. He stared at them through the windshield, as if begging them to run him over, to finish the deed someone else had started.

"Ohhh, my goodness. He's hurt." Chelsea's hand grasped the door handle.

"Chelsea, no."

She heard the anxiety in Trey's whispered warning and felt his hand brush her arm before she slipped from the truck. He was so full of worry; the man couldn't enjoy life. And all this concern about an injured puppy? This poor animal wasn't going to hurt her; he could barely stand up.

"Hey, sweet baby. Nobody's going to hurt you anymore," she cooed, moving closer. She smiled and knelt, holding out a hand for the dog to sniff.

She knew when Trey inched to crouch around her. The dog stiffened and bared his teeth. Let out a half-hearted growl. Poor thing.

Then she saw why the dog was upset. Trey had his gun drawn.

What was up with him?

She spun around and found her face practically snuggled against his neck. She gasped for air. He was so close. Close enough that she caught a hint of the coffee they'd shared earlier and a clean-smelling woodsy scent. Couldn't the man at least smell bad?

She couldn't think with him this close. Think? She couldn't breathe.

She pulled her face away from his neck, smiled and murmured soft words, not wanting to scare the dog further. "Trey, you need to put your gun away. He's nervous."

"Sorry. No can do. Even for a nervous wounded animal. We don't know how he got here." His whispered words fanned against her neck.

He was worried about an ambush? Didn't that only happen in the movies? She turned back to the dog. "It's OK, sweetheart. We're going to take you someplace safe."

She rubbed the dog's face, and he licked her fingers. Trey leaned around her to pet the dog with his free hand, enveloping her even more in his embrace.

"Trey, can you lift him into my truck?"

"Yeah, but I want you back in the cab first. I can't leave you out here unprotected."

"OK." She made to stand up, but he tugged her back down.

"With me. On the count of three. One. Two. Three."

They stood together with Trey's arms still around her, supporting her, protecting her. Wrapped in his arms felt nice, secure.

But this was his job. Wearing a badge. Protecting people. All kinds of people. Good and bad. The man lived and breathed danger.

She shrugged his arms from her shoulders and stomped to the truck. She didn't need his protection. The last thing she wanted to do was fall for a law enforcement officer again.

And falling for a marshal?

That ranked dead last.

❧

Trey rocked back and forth on his heels. Crouched over the dog, gun in hand, he watched Chelsea storm back to the truck. One minute she's nestling in his arms and he can barely keep his mind on his job, and the next she's snorting fire on her way to the truck.

He waited until she hopped into the cab. He didn't like sitting out in the open like this. But he especially didn't like the idea that someone had left a dog out here to die.

Someone who anticipated they would stop to rescue the animal?

Trey's stomach knotted, and he pulled out some antacids. He patted the dog. "Ready fella? Let's go see what happened to you."

Chelsea insisted on holding the dog all the way to the vet. The animal sprawled across her lap and spilled into the middle of the seat, hanging his droopy head towards Trey. He reached over to pet him. "He's obviously still in quite a bit of pain, but he looks pretty comfortable."

"Snuggles."

"Huh?"

"Snuggles. That's what I'm going to call him."

He rolled his eyes and gripped the steering wheel tighter. "Chelsea. It's a male dog. You can't name him Snuggles."

She glared at him. "Why not? That's what he wants to do."

Better go for a change of topic. Before he got in trouble by telling her he also enjoyed their snuggle back on the road. "Do animals naturally seem to seek you out?"

Her lips curved in that delicious way of hers. Tragedy averted.

"They always have. I suppose I should have been a vet." Chelsea stroked the dog's fur from his head all the way down his back, careful not to touch his wounded leg.

"Maybe. But I don't think you've wasted your energy or your talents as a guidance counselor. Teenagers can't seem to resist you, either."

That produced a full-fledged smile in his direction. *Way to go, Colten!*

"Remember that natural charm I warned you about?"

He threw back his head and laughed. "Yes. And after a few days in your presence, I'm inclined to agree with you."

He pulled into the veterinarian's parking lot and glanced her way, surprised to see her grinning. "What?"

"Saved by the vet."

Her words hit him like a piano dropping ten stories. She was flirting with him.

He took his time walking around to her side of the truck. He opened the door and leaned in, planting his hand on the seat next to her shapely legs. His face hovered inches from hers while he savored the way her wavy hair cascaded down her shoulders, the lips that curved in that always graceful way, and the eyes that spoke everything his heart wanted to hear.

Her eyes closed, and her lips parted slightly.

Trey snapped out of it. He couldn't do this. He was on the job. She didn't know the secrets he knew, the truth about her husband.

Her eyes startled open. As much as he wanted to partake and enjoy, he couldn't. He touched a silky curl framing her face and ran it through his fingers. "You need to know that right now I'm working. But there will come a time, soon, when I'm not."

8

Chelsea tuned her ears to the crackling of the campfire and the river cascading across rocks in the distance. A beautiful crescent moon began its path skyward and stars shimmered brightly overhead. The only way the night would be any brighter was if Jake were here.

She smiled at the firelight that flickered across exuberant youthful expressions, chocolate and marshmallow-smudged faces. S'mores. Who wouldn't want a s'more while sitting around a campfire?

Chelsea leaned back against a wide maple tree away from the ring of teenagers, closed her eyes, and heaved a contented sigh. She'd done what she set out to do with this get-together. The kids enjoyed the games she'd organized, and they devoured delicious hamburgers and hot dogs. She also chatted with each one individually to let them know about Journey's End. Now, it was Pastor Chris's turn to lead the devotion, a perfect way to end the evening.

Trey finished melting his marshmallows by the tiny fire ring and ambled her way, licking some chocolate from his graham cracker. He sat next to her, swinging his long, lean legs out and leaning back against the same tree. His shoulder brushed hers, and she scooted over to give him more room, admiring his brawny arms from under the guise of her smile.

Dependable. Strong. Protective. He was still in protection mode, even though she'd agreed to move the shindig from her place to the wooded lot behind Jamee and Ethan's house. The man never relaxed.

He leaned close to her ear. "Having fun?" he whispered.

"Absolutely.." She smiled and murmured back. "Are you?"

"Oh yeah. Never seen so many chocolate-covered faces in my life."

Chelsea glanced around the circle of teenagers, taking in each face engrossed in what Pastor Chris was saying. "So beautiful, aren't they? Children are such a blessing from God. At whatever stage of their development."

Trey grinned at her in the darkness, the firelight causing shadows to dance across his face. "My sister might not always say that. You should see my two-year-old twin nephews. Especially about this time every night when they have driven her to bed from sheer exhaustion."

Chelsea's eyes widened with envy. "Twin nephews? How lucky can a man be?"

"Yeah. The way they wear my sister out, though, they'll probably be my only ones."

"I don't have any nieces or nephews yet, and probably won't for a while. How do you keep from spoiling them to death?" Maybe Trey used his twin nephews as barbells instead of going to the gym. Whatever method he used to stay in shape, it was working. Definitely! Chelsea turned her head away from those arms. She needed a distraction. She zoned in on Pastor Chris, but it was useless. She turned back to Trey.

Trey finished eating his s'more, and his lips curled in a smile. "Well, I can't help but spoil them when I'm in town. But I'm out of town enough that they're not spoiled rotten. Nothing like having two of the little rugrats climb all over your lap."

Chelsea nodded. She could only imagine. Didn't Trey ever want any of his own?

"What about you?"

Drat! He caught her looking at his arms again, all corralled strength under control. Chelsea tore her gaze away from his arms and focused on his question. What had they been talking about? "What about me?"

"I know you have a brother. Do you have any sisters?"

"One brother and one sister. My younger sister, Cassidy, just got married last year and doesn't have any children yet. And my brother Carter will never get married. Or so he says," Chelsea added with a smile. She knew differently. Carter was a flirt. He just hadn't met the one who could hold his interest for longer than a couple months. "But, soon I'll have two babies to cuddle, Jamee's and Kalyn's. They will never have to pay a babysitter."

Trey laughed, and Chelsea shot a sideways glance at him. The moon, bright and looming low, served as his backdrop. She was enjoying his company. A lot. Way too much.

She blinked and swallowed hard. How had this happened? She lowered her head, ashamed that she hadn't thought about Doug much since Trey walked into her life.

Trey didn't wear a ring, and he hadn't mentioned a wife. An eligible good-looking man who helped in the kitchen, a strong man, yet gentle in spirit? What woman would pass that up?

Chelsea frowned. Maybe it was his job. Too much danger and definitely too much travel. Who wanted their husband to be gone for weeks at a time, protecting criminals? Or sons of criminals, in Jake's case.

Husband? She shook her head decisively. No way. She'd been down that road before. When Doug went undercover, sometimes she wouldn't see him for days. Weeks. It was too much. She wouldn't do it again. Nope. She didn't see her future with a gun-toting, badge-sporting cop of any kind.

She looked at him.

His eyes were closed.

"Trey?"

"Hmm?" His voice was soft, eyes still closed.

"Have you ever been married?" Did that sound like she was interested? She cringed, feeling her neck heat up. Well, was she? No. Definitely not. Not ever. It was just an opener for a nice, relaxing conversation.

Trey's head jerked off the tree, blue eyes popping open as if he'd been having a bad dream. He stared at her for what seemed like an eternity before he answered. "No. Not yet."

So much for their relaxed conversation. Good thing he didn't bolt upright with his gun drawn. "Just haven't met the right one? Or is that too personal for a marshal to answer?"

"I've met the right woman. Just not at the right time."

"Oh." Chelsea didn't know why she suddenly felt disappointed, deflated. Why her heart dropped to her stomach.

Trey continued, looking straight at Chelsea,

although the glare of the moonlight hid his face. "I travel a lot. And I'm under a lot of stress. Usually always surrounded by a good bit of danger. What woman wants to commit to live with all of that?"

She could sense him studying her face in the darkness. Intently. What could she say? She knew she didn't want that kind of relationship.

Or did she?

Chelsea lowered her eyes. She understood the ever-present dangers of being married to an undercover cop. And the stress that he was sometimes unable to leave at the door when quitting time rolled around. But, there was no quitting time for an undercover cop, or in Trey's case, a Deputy U.S. Marshal.

"Someone who loves you, for sure. Someone who is willing to accept the dangers inherent in your profession. You'll find that someone."

Trey remained silent for a minute, almost brooding. "I don't really want anyone else. If the right time never comes around or it doesn't ever work out, then it'll be just me. For thirty-five years now, it's been just me. I'm not settling for anyone else."

"Wow. That's some lucky woman."

He had bared his soul. Why was she disappointed? Every heart searched for their soul mate. That one special person whom God made uniquely just for them, who made them complete. Perhaps one day, the woman would overlook Trey's occupation and love just the man.

9

Trey jerked upright in bed at the shrill alarm piercing the night.

He threw off the heavy comforter and quickly pulled on jeans, grabbing his radio and gun from the nightstand on the way out. The shirt could wait. And the shoes.

He met Chelsea in the hallway, gun in one of her hands while she silenced the alarm.

"Whoa, Chelsea! What's with the gun?"

Her curly hair was tousled and her eyes were soft from sleep. It was enough for him to lower his gun. Only for a moment, though. His guard went back up. He noted that she didn't lower her own weapon.

"Protection. Doug insisted I know how to protect myself. And others."

"Forget about it," Trey whispered. "Stay here."

Trey went down the stairway confident that Chelsea would stay behind. But now he had a new problem, a gun-toting female following him, determination lining her lips, gun still tight in her hand.

"The security alarm shows a breech at the dining room window."

He didn't need the distraction of her whispered words near his ear. How was he supposed to protect her? "Is the window open?"

"It doesn't indicate that the window is open. The security system is ultra sensitive. It could be that someone tried to open it or just got too close to it."

"Chelsea, stay upstairs. I'll take care of it."

She scowled and continued following him down the steps, her gun pointed towards the floor. "Not on your life, buddy. You don't have to worry about me. I can take care of myself. Nobody's breaking in to my place."

He took the steps ahead of her, quietly speaking into the radio. "P-one, come in."

"One here."

"The security alarm is sounding. It appears we've had some type of breech from the dining room window. Did you see anything?"

"Negative."

"Move in tighter to the house. Inspect the perimeter before coming in. We'll cover more ground that way faster. Give us some warning before coming inside, though."

Trey reached the bottom of the steps and leveled his gun. He flipped the light switch on. If someone was inside, he had the advantage of knowing the layout of the house.

He scanned the great room, his gun following the path his eyes took. Chelsea's breath warmed his bare arm. Why hadn't she stayed upstairs like he asked?

He gestured towards the dining room for her to follow, but she took off in the other direction. What was she doing? He bit his tongue to keep from yelling out at her. He'd make sure they had words later.

He moved into the dining room. She went through the nook where the pool table sat, and they met in the dining room. He noted her gun wasn't pointing directly at him, but it was close enough that she only had to shift slightly to target him, or an intruder. Obviously, a professional trained her. *Doug.*

Two windows, one on either side of the dining room, remained shut.

"Kitchen," he whispered, hearing a pint-sized bark coming from the utility room.

She nodded and followed him, lowering her gun. She leaned forward and spoke softly in his ear. "The alarm showed dining room. I don't think we'll find anybody in the kitchen if the windows are still shut."

"They could have closed the window behind them. You have too many nooks in the kitchen not to check."

She nodded, her tousled curls bouncing. "Right behind you."

His radio squawked. "P-one at the back door."

"Ten-four. We're in the kitchen. Don't come in shooting."

Trey and Chelsea swept the kitchen, checking the pantry and closet. Nothing. Trey lowered his gun, relief sweeping over him in waves. He reached to unlock the back door to allow the agent entry.

Rogers poked his head through the back door, gun drawn. "Anything?"

"Nada." He turned around, noticed the warmth had disappeared from the room. His heart plummeted to his stomach. "Where'd Chelsea go?"

He raced back into the dining room and stopped cold. Chelsea stood staring out into the black night, the drapes pulled back, the window open.

He couldn't think past the sudden rush of emotion that flooded his body. His job was to protect her at all costs, including his own life. Taking a deep breath, he

sprinted towards her.
"Chelsea!"

10

The air left Chelsea's body in a *thwump*, stunning her so she couldn't breathe. She lay motionless for a second, willing her lungs to fill up. As tackles went, Trey's had been incredibly gentle, with one of his arms reaching behind to break their fall, the other cradling her around the waist. Both of his arms now had her pinned to the floor underneath his muscular body. He would be lucky to escape with no broken bones. What would she be lucky to escape with? Her heart intact?

"Flag!...Where are the refs...when you need them?" She croaked under his weight.

A low rumble started at his throat. Was it a growl or a chuckle?

"That was...quite a tackle. I think...you might have missed...your calling."

He leaned back so his face was directly in front of hers. He worked his jaw, clenching it tight. She could sense the fear radiating from his body. He wasn't smiling.

She started to shake, but not from the adrenaline. And not because she was frightened. She hadn't been this close to a man in three years. She reached a hand up to touch his face.

"A sniper wouldn't have missed that shot." He spoke through gritted teeth. His voice sounded shaky against her ear. "Are you OK?"

She jerked her hand back and frowned at his harsh tone. He was only doing his job. He didn't actually care about her. She squirmed at the pressure under her back. "I think so. Except for something hard behind my back."

He lifted her gently with one hand and pulled his gun out, placing it on the table next to them. "Sorry."

She expected he would help her up then, but he didn't. The other arm slid back around her waist, keeping her wrapped close to him.

She closed her eyes. Why did it feel so right to be in his arms? How could his arms fit around her perfectly, his body melded to hers as if they belonged together? She felt protected, safe, like he would never allow anything to hurt her. She opened her eyes and saw the gun on the table.

No, this wasn't good. Not good at all. She barely knew him. And he was a marshal. She'd do best to remember that important little detail.

She heard a door shut in the kitchen and Snuggles crying in the utility room where she had nestled him for the night. Too much excitement for the poor dog. Who was she kidding? It was too much excitement for her.

"It was just a deer, Trey. I saw him. He probably got a little too close to the window. I told you my security system was good. Maybe a little too sensitive." *Like me.* She willed herself to stop shaking.

"Chelsea, you can't take chances like that. Don't you know…"

A trace of cigarette smoke wafted through the window. Chelsea heard a muffled thump outside. Footsteps pounded hard through the darkness.

Trey scrambled to his knees and grabbed his radio,

peering outside through the bottom corner of the window. He motioned for her to stay on the floor. "Rogers. What's your status?"

No response.

"Chelsea. Stay inside. Keep the doors locked. Keep away from the windows. I'm going out to check on Rogers." Trey's words came out terse, clipped.

"But—"

Chelsea struggled to get off the floor so she could go with Trey. What was going on outside? She reached for her gun.

"Chelsea. Please. Stay inside."

Those pleading blue eyes were all it took. And the memory of his arms holding her tight.

☙⤫

Chelsea held the back door open, Snuggles tucked under her arm, his warmth helping to calm her nerves.

Trey grabbed the wet paper towels she handed him and bent to scrub the bottoms of his bare feet. "Thanks. And thanks for listening this time."

She got it. The unspoken message that she hadn't followed orders the first time. "What did you find? Or should I say who?"

"His name is Jimmie Charles. Mean anything to you?" He studied her face.

She thought for a minute. "No. Should it?"

"Not especially. He works for Carpocelli's mob."

"So you were right."

Trey stood up and dropped the dirty towels in the trash can. His lowered head spoke volumes about her doubt. "He worked for your construction crew. That's one of the reasons Carpocelli's mob contacted him.

They knew he would know the layout of your house."

"Oh, dear God." Chelsea set Snuggles on a towel in the utility room. "I checked their backgrounds, references, licensing. Wh-what more could I have done?" She hung her head and closed her eyes, allowing the tears swelling in her eyes to trickle down her cheeks.

Trey framed her face with his hands, and she opened her eyes. His thumbs gently swabbed at her tears. "It's OK, Chelsea. We got him before he did anything...terrible."

"Was he the same one that visited before? When you and I were out walking?"

"Mmm-hmm."

She reached up and kissed him on the cheek—just a peck—and then backed away from his tender grasp. Best to keep a little distance tonight, while her emotions were fully charged. "Thank you. I'm glad you guys were here. But you know I can take care of myself."

He smiled with gentle eyes and stepped towards her. "So you keep saying."

She backed away, but the washing machine halted her progress. She needed to get out of this tight space before she did something stupid like play with the hairs on his chest or run her hands up his arms until they wound around his neck. Yeah. Something really stupid.

He grabbed a clean folded t-shirt off the washing machine and slipped it over his head.

She stepped around him to the kitchen, frustration and relief warring heavily in her heart. Snuggles hobbled behind her. "I made some hot chocolate for everybody. Where is Rogers?"

"He'll be coming in a second. He's just briefing Jenkins."

She ladled the chocolate, squirted some whip cream on top and handed him the steaming mug.

He took a sip and his lips curved in a wicked grin. "It's good. But not as good as mine."

She laughed, exhaustion making her lose her senses, forget who she was dealing with and why. For the first time in three years, someone made her feel alive, beautiful, flirtatious. She took the dishtowel in her hands and playfully swatted him with it. "What a tease!"

Snuggles yapped once, but she hardly noticed. Trey lifted his mug to keep it from spilling. He set the mug on the counter and took a step towards her. Maybe to finish what he started earlier? Or what she wanted him to start?

She saw his eyes darken. Gone was the playfulness, replaced with something different. Something tender. Soft. She took a step in his direction.

Agent Rogers cleared his throat and they both jumped. "Excuse me. I'm heading out now. It should be a quiet night now with Charles in custody. He knows that Jake isn't here which means Carpocelli knows. Everybody can relax."

Relax? Who could relax? Everybody except her, maybe. Not with Trey Colten, Deputy U.S. Marshal, staying in her house.

ॐॐ

Relax? How could he relax? Sheer exhaustion should have taken over long ago. Trey stared at the ceiling. Glanced at the alarm clock. Four a.m. He tossed the pillow from his bed, joining the other one already on the floor.

Why hadn't he jumped on that vacation when he had the chance?

Every time he closed his eyes, he pictured Chelsea, her hair billowing gently with the breeze. Felt the way her warm body molded perfectly to his. Could still make out the barest hint of chocolate from when she kissed his cheek.

And he still felt his heart lurch to the floor after hearing footsteps pounding outside.

The thought of what Charles had planned chilled him to the core. Instructions Carpocelli wanted carried out to the letter.

He couldn't let her have this effect on him. How could he protect her with his heart in knots?

Well. It wouldn't matter now. Hamilton told him last night when he reported the incident that the danger to Chelsea should be over. He was to stay with her today, and then check in to the safe house tomorrow.

And he still hadn't had the perfect opportunity to talk to her about Doug. Why hadn't he had the courage to be the one to break the news after the sting went sour? Or for that matter, for the three years he'd gone to see her at the memorial gardens? Why hadn't he stayed after Doug's parents left and talked to her privately? Why hadn't he bared his heart, told her what he knew about her husband's death? Begged forgiveness for his part?

Because he didn't know he would be in her house. Protecting her. And actually relishing the job.

That's why.

She would hate him. Hate him. Hate him. He

drifted…

Trey glanced at the clock beside the bed and groaned. Five a.m. Although his body complained about yesterday's physical activities, his mind wouldn't rest. He kept replaying the conversation with Chelsea when he told her that he had found the right woman. She seemed…disappointed?

He jerked off the covers. He might as well get up.

He'd blown it last night. He had no choice but to answer Chelsea's questions honestly, the time for evasiveness and omission long past. As much as he hated the thought, he needed to tell her the truth soon.

He pulled on jeans and a t-shirt and went downstairs, trying not to wake her. Or Snuggles. He smiled and pushed the button to start the coffeemaker. Snuggles. What a name. He prepped Molly's bottle while he waited for the beloved brew to drip.

Chelsea was right. He was thirty-five years old. He was ready to marry and settle down. He yearned for more days at home. To enjoy being at home after work, maybe having some friends over for a barbecue or picnic. To round up enough players for an impromptu scrimmage football game. Or just to relax in the great room or on the front porch reading the newspaper. To savor weekends like he had this weekend. To have someone to come home to.

He wanted Chelsea. But, right now wasn't the right time, not in the middle of this mess with Carpocelli. Would there ever be a right time for them?

Maybe. Once he told her the truth about her husband's death. Then, when, and if, she was able to forgive him…then, maybe.

And he had to make peace with God. After spending the last few days with Chelsea, he felt God's nudging to restore their relationship. Pastor Chris's words last night on truth and healing had touched his heart. Until Trey asked God for forgiveness, he would never be whole or healed. It was time to stop questioning "why" and accept that he might not ever know the "whys" this side of Heaven.

Trey looked at his watch. Chelsea wouldn't be up for another hour. He poured coffee into a to-go cup, scribbled a note telling her where he would be, and left it on the counter where she would see it first thing.

He opened the utility room door and scooped up the whimpering pup. "Come on, Snuggles. Let's go for a walk."

Balancing cup and pup, he opened the back door and scanned the property. Nothing moved but the squawking ducks.

"That's a good sign, buddy. Maybe today will be quiet. What do you think?" He walked to the barn, his gaze sliding in all directions. All clear.

He released Snuggles to do his business while he fed Molly.

"How's my sweet girl this morning?" Trey stroked the fawn's fur. He'd miss this eclectic mix of animals.

And their mistress. He gave Molly's head one last scratch. "You'll miss her too, girl, won't you?"

Trey closed the barn and scanned the area. A nice long walk would help the anxiety building in his gut.

"Let's go, buddy." He scooped Snuggles, tucked him under one arm, and then hiked to the riverbank.

"There you go, little fella." He released Snuggles to hobble around on his cast. "Don't go far."

Trey settled onto a large rock. The sun hadn't made itself visible yet, and in the semi-darkness a heavy mist hovered, suspended slightly above the water's reach. He could hear more than see the little ripples lapping over the rocks.

The scene gripped his heart. So peaceful and gentle, and yet displayed the power of God through its majesty. How could he have drifted so far from this God of love?

Trey took a long sip of his coffee and in the eerie stillness of the morning, prayed.

God, I'm so sorry. Please forgive me. I've been so arrogant. I've taken a situation like Doug's death and because I had no answers, I created my own. Truly ignorant responses like You weren't there for Doug. That You aren't there for me. But, I know that's not true. According to Your promise, You will never leave us or forsake us. You were there for Doug, You've been with Chelsea all along, and You're here for me. Even though I surely don't deserve it. Thank You for bringing Chelsea here, for providing good friends for her, and for allowing her time to heal. Thank You for Your healing grace.

God, why didn't I talk to her at Doug's funeral? Why didn't I tell her the truth, then? Now, I feel like it's too late. But, I know the truth is never too late and it will heal my heart, set me free. Help her to forgive me when I tell her. Help me to forgive myself. Thank You for loving me even when I'm unlovable. Help me to be the man You created me to be. And, if it's in Your will, help me to be the man Chelsea deserves to have.

You're such a loving God. How could I have strayed so far and stayed away so long? Help me never to abandon You again.

Trey lifted his head and felt a hundred pounds lighter. His fatigue and anxiety had slowly seeped away during his prayer, along with the fear and bitterness he had harbored the last three years. With

God's help, he could do this. He would do this. He would tell Chelsea the truth.

Before he left tomorrow.

She needed to know the truth about her husband and even more, he needed to confess. Their relationship could never progress if he wasn't truthful. Could he trust God that telling her would not destroy whatever thread of feelings he felt growing?

Thunder rumbled in the distance. Trey looked up at the sky and noticed murky gray clouds moving in, shadows now filtered through to the ground. Treetops swayed in tune with the wind.

A twig snapped nearby. Twisting his head sharply, he reached for his gun. When he saw Snuggles hobbling his way, whimpering, he relaxed slightly, loosening his grip on the cold steel.

"Afraid of a little thunder, hey, boy?" He hopped down from the rock and reached out his hand to pet the pooch.

Suddenly, a streak of lightning snapped a tree branch off to their side, sending white-hot sparks and pieces of timber debris flying in the air over their heads.

"I guess it's time for us to head back, little fella."

Time for confession.

11

"Chelsea."

"Hmm?" Her gaze never left the television, glued to the car race she'd taped. He set Snuggles down.

Maybe now wasn't a good time.

Snuggles limped in front of Chelsea, and then sat facing the television. Crazy pup. Looked like he was watching the race. Chelsea stroked under the lab's chin.

Trey watched the cars speed around the track. Someone edged up into another driver, causing him to spin around and hit the wall. The caution flag went up. Everybody would be heading for pit stops. A break in the action.

Maybe on TV. But not in here.

"Chelsea. Can you stop the race for a few minutes? I need to talk to you."

She blinked. "Sure." She flicked the TV off. "Are you leaving?"

Surprise. Surprise. He rated higher than a race.

Was that disappointment clouding her eyes? Maybe he ought to use the opportunity to lighten the moment. Before he dropped the bomb. "Already missing my captivating company?"

She giggled and threw a pillow at him. "No. I'm still trying to get rid of you. Can't you see that?"

"Playful this morning, eh?" He sank down on the

other end of the couch and scowled, hating to ruin the moment.

Chelsea tilted her head to the side. "What's up with you? Didn't you enjoy your morning off?"

He shrugged. "What morning off?"

"You weren't tagging around behind me like every other morning, getting in the way. You didn't sit outside with me. I assumed you took the morning off."

She had missed his company.

"I talked to Hamilton last night. After the incident with Charles."

She drew her knees up and grabbed another throw pillow, cradling it against her chest. Snuggles plopped down with a huff and curled up. "And?"

"He feels the danger threat for you is over. He wants me to catch up with Renner and Jake tomorrow." Not exactly what he wanted to tell her first, but she'd broached the topic.

"Just when I was starting to get used to having you around." He didn't miss the sudden droop in her shoulders, the dimming of her normally thousand-watt smile. "I kind of like waking up to freshly-made coffee."

He smiled, but his heart wasn't in it. He wasn't ready to leave either. He wanted to explore...Who was he kidding?

He was leaving tomorrow, so he had precious little time left with her. Even less when Kalyn woke up and came downstairs. He'd better get with it. "Chelsea, I have a confession to make. Will you listen to me even when it gets tough and it seems like you can't listen anymore?" *Chelsea, listen to my heart. Focus on my heart.*

She uncoiled long legs and leaned towards him, dropping the pillow to her side. The dog flicked his ears back as if knowing the news wasn't good. "I think so."

Trey's phone buzzed at his waist, drawing him away from Chelsea's wide eyes. He snapped it from the clip. "It's Renner. I have to take this. I'll be right back."

He hoisted himself off the couch and accepted the call while he walked into the pool room. From the corner of his eyes, he saw Chelsea head towards the kitchen, Snuggles limping along behind her. "Hey. How's it going?"

"Are you sitting down?"

Frustration rippled through his gut. Here it was confession time, and Renner was playing games with him. "No. I'm pacing. Just like I do every time I talk to you. What's up?"

"Jake's disappeared."

His stomach roiled and he grabbed the antacids out of his pocket. "Disappeared? How? What happened? Did somebody snatch him?"

"Stop with the twenty questions already. I'll explain everything when you get here. The bottom line is we think he took off for Raleigh. For his mom's funeral."

Trey raked a hand through his hair, willing this case to be over. For an end to Carpocelli and his evil.

He saw Chelsea doing a little pacing herself, back and forth, from the coffeepot to the island in the middle of the kitchen. Still holding the phone to his ear, he stared at her, allowing her charisma to sweep over him like spring's first rain. That same allure of hers attracted teenagers and animals alike. She was light compared to his darkness, summer to his winter, peace to his...job.

What did he have to offer her?

Nothing but pain.

Trouble.

A badge.

If this phone call wasn't a "not yet" from God, he didn't know what was.

Thank you, God.

ॐ

Something was dreadfully wrong. Chelsea felt it right down to her bones.

Had Carpocelli snatched Jake from the marshals? She traded the coffee mugs for to-go cups and hurried back into the great room, Snuggles following her so close, she could feel his muzzle against her heels.

Thunder rumbled, and lightning flashed right outside the window. Jake was out there somewhere.

Chelsea sat down on the edge of the couch, tapping her foot on the floor, and waited for Trey to disconnect the call. What was taking so long? Maybe she should tell Kalyn she'd be leaving for awhile? But then Trey might leave without her. No, best just wait until he got off the phone and could explain.

Finally, he placed the cell phone in the clip and raked a hand through his hair. Swallowed two more antacids. Trudged back to where she sat, waiting, stroking Snuggles.

She cleared her throat, unwilling to let him know how scared she was for Jake. "Is something wrong?"

His Adam's apple bobbed a couple times. "Renner says that Jake's disappeared. They think he's heading to Raleigh. For his mother's funeral."

She should have known. All the poor kid wanted

to do was say goodbye to his mama. She should have chatted with him and discussed plans before he left, but she'd been caught unaware during the night. Wouldn't happen next time. "So when do we leave?"

His head whipped around so fast he sputtered coffee on the dog. "We?"

"You don't think I'm going to sit at home twiddling my thumbs while Jake is out there"—she jerked her head to the window just as lightning flashed—"somewhere, do you?"

"I know you won't be twiddling your thumbs..." He grinned, a teasing twist to his lips. He dipped his head to Snuggles resting at her feet. "Probably more like drumming up teenagers or tracking down wounded animals or feeding your baby deer or those squawking ducks."

He had her there. She did have a lot to do. But she couldn't leave Jake in the lurch. Not when he needed her. "I'll go tell Kalyn we're leaving. She can take care of Snuggles and Molly and the ducks for me."

Trey shook his head slowly.

The rat.

"Trey, I can help you. He just wants to say goodbye to his mama. Let me talk to him. That's my job, remember? Counseling?" Chelsea plastered her most pleading look on her face. "Besides, you can't up and leave me without protection, can you? Aren't you supposed to stay with me today?"

He narrowed eyes at her, drew his lips into a thin line. "Hamilton doesn't feel you're in danger anymore."

"Maybe he doesn't. But you do."

At the slight flaring of his nostrils and the muscle tensing in his jaw, Chelsea knew she had him. She set her coffee cup down and headed for the stairs. "I'm going to go grab a couple things and tell Kalyn what's going on. I'll be right down. Don't leave without me."

"Chelsea."

One softly spoken word and she stopped, turned around. What was it about Trey that set her heart on fire? Her nerves to tingling? "Yes?"

"On one condition."

Uh-oh. "What's that?"

"You stay where I tell you to stay. Do what I tell you to do. It's too dangerous for you to go to the funeral. I don't want you anywhere near there."

Well, that was tying her hands, wasn't it? "But, Trey, how am I supposed to counsel Jake if I'm not there when you find him?"

"That's the deal. Take it or leave it."

If that's what it took for her to help Jake, that's what she'd do. She nodded. "OK."

Suspicion tightened around his lips and his eyebrows dipped in the center. "OK? Just like that?"

She chuckled at his incredulous tone. "What? Were you expecting a fight?"

He laughed. She liked his laugh. Kind of like that first jolt of caffeine in the morning when it slides down. Smooth. Rich. Full of flavor. "Yes. And you know it."

"Well, sorry to disappoint you."

He cocked one eyebrow and grasped each of her shoulders. "Chelsea, don't ever think you could disappoint me."

OK. She'd have to come back to that comment later. After she'd had time to digest it. "I have one condition, too."

He backed up, releasing his hold on her. "You're not in any position to be making demands."

She ignored him. And also ignored her shoulders tingling from the effect of his hands. "At least let me see Jake before we leave Raleigh."

He scrubbed his hands across the stubble on his cheeks.

"Where would you like me to stay while you and Renner are out looking for Jake?"

He raked a hand through his hair. "We'll discuss it on the way. Go grab a couple changes of clothes and tell Kalyn we'll be leaving. Do you think Kalyn could have a friend stay with her until you get back?"

"I'm sure under the circumstances she wouldn't mind. I'll tell her. Do you think I might be able to see my family while we're there?"

He nodded slowly. "I'm sure we can manage that."

"Good. Then that's settled."

12

Not exactly where she had in mind to stay while she waited for Trey and Renner to track down Jake, but, hey, who could resist twins?

She watched four little arms squeeze Trey's legs. Reaching down, he scooped up two little giggling bodies while his sister, Peyton, looped an arm around his waist.

"Hey, buddies. What mischief have you two been up to lately?" Trey snuggled his face deep into both of their chests so that his overnight bag fell from his shoulder. Chelsea bent down to pick it up and did a double take at the transformation on his face, softening from the gruff expression he wore the entire trip to a gentleness immediately upon seeing his sister and her twins.

Did he regret bringing her here? Since loading in her truck for the two-hour drive, Trey had hardly spoken two words. Well, actually, five. "You'll stay at my sister's."

Trey turned around with the two little bodies still wrapped around his waist and smiled. "Chelsea, this is my sister, Peyton, and her two munchkins Matthew and Zachary. Peyton, Chelsea."

She turned to smile and shook the other woman's hand. "Hi, Peyton. It's nice to meet you. And your boys. They're beautiful."

"Thank you."

Chelsea stared from one twin to the other. "But how do you tell them apart?"

Peyton smiled, love for her children settling in her gaze as she glanced at each child. "Matthew is the one wearing blue pants. Zachary has the red ones on. Once you get to know them, though, you'll recognize the differences in their personalities."

Both kids were absolute cherubs with a sprinkling of Trey's dark hair, but lighter blue eyes, instead of his intense color. Somewhat mischievous cherubs, she thought, as she saw Matthew pinch Trey's chin dimple with all the force he could muster.

"Trey has told us so much about you, Chelsea. After the way he raved about how scrumptious your cooking is, I have to say I'm a little jealous. When he told us about your brownies, I repented about my hard feelings right then. It's been a long time since I made homemade brownies." Peyton eyed the wiggle worms wrapped around Trey and winked. "Especially in the last couple of years."

Chelsea couldn't stop a laugh from bubbling out. She liked Peyton. Anyone that brutally honest...how could she not? "I don't know how you would ever find the time to bake with two active two year olds."

Peyton planted hands on hips. "Yeah, well, honestly I don't know how I find time to get dressed in the morning. These two keep me busy all day long. They are into everything. When I crawl into bed at night, I fall asleep from exhaustion. My husband says at this rate we'll never have the little girl we'd like."

Chelsea laughed, making a mental note. Anything she might say about Trey could be used against her at a later date.

Trey disengaged gently from the two little boys and they scattered off to parts of the house unknown. Peyton's house was comfortable, littered with children's toys in the great room.

Just the way hers would be one day.

"I hate to leave so soon, Peyt, but I have to meet up with Renner. We've got a situation to resolve." He wasn't happy. The hard line of his jaw and the stubborn set of his chin said he wished the situation was over. "After we get things settled, I'm going to check on Mom, too."

"Do you want to bring Mom over?"

He thought for a minute, and then shook his head. "I better not."

Peyton glanced at Chelsea. "Mom has MS. She has good days and bad days. She lives with Trey in his condo."

"Oh, I'm sorry. I don't mean to be in the way." Chelsea's words strangled in her throat, her selfish desire to visit her parents coming back to haunt her.

Trey shook his head. "You're not in the way. Mom has a caregiver around when I'm not in town so we know she's taken care of. She'll be all right. I just want to stop in and say hi."

"OK. You go ahead. Chelsea and I will get to know each other. And if I'm lucky, maybe she'll show me how to make those brownies." Peyton grinned mischievously at her brother.

Trey's mouth twisted into his lopsided smile. "Peyt, it will take a lot more than Chelsea *showing* you how to make her brownies for them to be that good. She'll have to *make* them for you, too. If I recall the last time you baked brownies, the whole pan had to be thrown out."

Peyton pretended a hurt expression and playfully punched her brother in the arm. "Thanks, Trey, for remembering my last miserable escapade into the culinary world of baking. You know I do much better at, uh, um, ah…"

Trey rolled his eyes. "Just face it, Peyton. If it weren't for takeout, you guys wouldn't eat."

Chelsea narrowed her eyes at him. "Didn't you have to be somewhere?"

"Are you trying to get rid of me so soon?" Trey drawled. "After I so readily agreed to bring you here?"

Chelsea sputtered and threw her hands in the air. "Trey, you need to go find Ja—"

Trey stepped back with his palms in surrender position. "All right. All right. I'm going." He turned to his sister. "Peyton, make sure you keep all the doors locked. I hope to be here by dinnertime. I have my cell if you need me."

"Sure."

Nobody said anything for a full sixty seconds. This was awkward.

Chelsea hung her head. She really wanted to say goodbye to Trey in private. But, how could she say that to Trey's sister without appearing rude?

Trey cleared his throat and gave his sister one of those looks. She took the hint. "I think I'll go see what the kids are up to."

Chelsea didn't turn her head to acknowledge Peyton. Her eyes were glued to Trey, studying the creases around his eyes, the deep cleft in his chin, the slight slant of his lips. The sparkle in his eyes as he looked back at her.

She wanted him to leave so he could find Jake.

She wanted him to stay. For her.

"I've got to go."

Of course he did.

"This is for Jake." Chelsea handed the bag to Trey.

"What's in it?" He opened the bag before she answered, pulling out a long haired wig, letting it dangle from his fingertips like it was a germ for the dreaded flu. "What…"

"Some of my hus…Doug's toys for his undercover jobs. So Jake can attend his mama's funeral."

He set the wig on the hall table and peered into the bag, rummaging through the contents with his free hand. "You want him to dress up like a woman?" He snorted and rolled his eyes. "In case you hadn't noticed, counselor, Jake's already got facial hair."

"I figured you'd say that. That's why I packed the shaver and the five minute hair color."

He grimaced. "And what would that be for?"

"Shave his head, give him a buzz cut. Then use that quick acting color on his hair and his eyebrows. Throw in the eyeglasses. He'll look like a different kid."

He tossed everything back in the bag, including the wig. "Sounds like we'd need a lot of time for that."

"You got a better idea, marshal?" She flashed the don't-mess-with-me look she reserved for some of her more difficult students.

"Can't say that I do, ma'am." His palm, hardened and calloused, cupped her cheek in a tender and protective gesture. He brushed an errant curl behind her ear, his fingers sliding through her hair and settling on her shoulder.

She leaned in closer, waiting, hoping, wanting.

"Chelsea, I…" His grip tightened.

A squeal erupted from the other room.

Abruptly he stepped back, releasing her so fast she wobbled forward. "We'll find him. Don't worry." Frowning, he turned away from her and bolted out the front door.

Disappointment coupled with fear tightened like a snake around Chelsea's heart. She locked the door and felt the tears welling while she leaned her forehead against the cool metal. *Please let them find Jake before something terrible happens to him. To any of them.*

She wouldn't cry. Not in front of his sister and the babies. She willed the tears away, swiped at the moisture accumulating around her eyes.

You're such an idiot, Chelsea. How many times does he have to remind you that he's a marshal? He's only doing his job.

She would not fall for someone in law enforcement. She would not fall for someone in law enforcement. She would not fall for someone in law enforcement.

If she told herself this enough times, it would be true, wouldn't it?

Chelsea peeled her forehead away from the closed front door to find Peyton smiling at her.

"He's not that bad."

She sniffled, stiffened. "What?"

"My brother. He's not that bad," Peyton repeated, still with that silly grin plastered on her face.

Just where Chelsea didn't want to go. She absolutely did not want to discuss Trey Colten right now. Maybe not ever. She lifted her chin, and crossed her arms. "You said you wanted help with dinner? Why don't you show me your kitchen and we'll see what we can cook up?"

While Peyton laid the twins down for their nap, Chelsea followed Peyton's instructions and scrounged through the freezer for something to make. Judging by the contents of the freezer and the refrigerator, Trey was right. Takeout was definitely on the menu a lot.

Peyton returned to the kitchen and crossed to the fridge. "Would you like some iced tea?"

"Sure. That'd be great. Thanks."

Peyton plopped some ice into the glasses and poured the tea. "I would love to see your place. Trey says it's an oasis out in the middle of nowhere. He speaks very highly of it. It sounds absolutely beautiful."

Chelsea nodded. She'd only lived at Journey Creek a little over a year but already she loved it there. "It is beautiful. Peaceful and serene." Her eyes narrowed. "At least it was, up until a few days ago. Trey and Renner brought a little excitement."

She opened the pantry door and scanned the shelves for something to fix with the ham she'd found in the fridge. Deciding on sweet potatoes and green beans, she pulled out both cans and shut the door.

Peyton grinned and handed her a glass of iced tea before sitting down at one of the bar stools at the counter. "I knew it. He's really turned your world upside-down, hasn't he?"

Chelsea nodded, opening the can of green beans. "Yes, but not in the way you think, Peyton."

Peyton had a puzzled look on her soft features, one eyebrow raised in question.

"I'm a casualty of sorts. Trey's just doing his job right now. He's protecting me." To say those thoughts aloud made Chelsea sad. Did she wish it to be more than that? She frowned.

Peyton leaned elbows on the kitchen counter, expression shadowed with concern. "What on earth happened?"

Chelsea debated what she could tell Peyton without breaking any confidentiality laws. "Long story. But the gist of it is, I just opened a shelter for troubled teens and my first arrival happened to be a teen who witnessed a federal crime. We called in the marshals because he wants to testify." Chelsea mixed the ingredients for a sweet potato casserole. "So, you see, I'm just Trey's job, right now. Nothing more."

Peyton's eyes clouded. "I'm sure he's worried about trouble arriving at your doorstep. Especially with your place so far out from anywhere." Her face cleared, and she smiled at Chelsea. "He takes his job very seriously, as I'm sure you've noticed."

Oh, yeah. She noticed too many things about Trey she had no business noticing. She glanced at the clock on the wall above the fridge. He'd been gone only an hour, but it felt like a week. "Tell me about your mother. How long has she had MS?"

"About ten years. In the beginning it wasn't so bad. She could move around without help most of the time." Peyton took a swig of iced tea.

"I guess now it's a lot worse?"

Peyton grimaced and tucked a strand of hair behind her ear. "Yeah. Most days she's in a wheelchair. She was in the hospital last month with pneumonia and it was touch and go for awhile. Trey took a lot of time off work. I don't think his boss liked that too much."

Chelsea scraped the sweet potatoes off the spatula into the casserole dish. How could his boss have a problem with Trey taking time off to be with his mother in the hospital? Didn't he understand how important family was?

"Anyway, Trey never says, but sometimes the stress of his job eats at him."

Chelsea covered the casserole with aluminum foil before putting it in the fridge to bake later. "With a boss like that, I can imagine."

"Yeah." Peyton sighed, standing up to rummage around the pantry. She held up a bag of chocolate chip cookies.

Chelsea nodded and sat down on the other stool. She picked up the tea glass and let the cool liquid slide down her throat. "Mmm." She nibbled a cookie. Kalyn would make fun of her. "My family lives here in Raleigh. Trey said I could see them while I was here."

"Really?" Peyton's surprise mingled with pleasure in her voice. "You're from around here?"

"Actually, I grew up in Raleigh. I didn't move to the Charlotte area until a year ago. After my husband died I couldn't bear to stay here any longer."

Peyton gulped, and her eyes filled with moisture. "You lost your husband? How sad. I'm so sorry."

Chelsea covered Peyton's hand lying on the counter and squeezed. "It's OK. God has been very good to me. These last three years have been very healing. Especially after moving away."

Peyton smiled. "You're a Christian." More a statement than a question.

"Yes, I am. Although I went through a tough time after my husband died. Too many questions and not enough answers. But God helped me through it and every day is a new day." God had whispered those words to Chelsea, morning after morning, just to help her get out of bed.

"We're Christians, too. Trey has been going through a rough patch, but I know he's dedicated to the Lord. He just has to find his way back."

Chelsea blinked. She'd seen Trey's inner struggle the last few days. He would tell her about it when he was ready.

When.

If.

OK. Maybe never.

Peyton set her empty glass on the counter, her expression dark. "About three years ago Trey handled a particularly traumatic case. He never talked about it but every time we saw him, he got more and more morose. One day he just stopped going to church. He hasn't been the same since."

"Really?" Chelsea's faith in God was what got her through her husband's death. What could have happened to Trey that made his faith flounder? And did this have anything to do with the woman he met? If it did, why didn't Peyton say anything about her?

Chelsea lowered her head. If Trey hadn't told his sister about this mysterious female, she wasn't about to break his confidence. Or ask.

"Yeah. For years, he worked in the Drug Trafficking Task Force. One case in particular got to him for whatever reason and he made the switch to Witness Protection almost immediately. I don't think he's regretted the move." Peyton glanced at her meaningfully. "Especially not now."

Three years ago. Drug Trafficking. That's odd. Chelsea sucked in a breath, ignoring Peyton's pointed look. She had already told Peyton that Trey wasn't interested in her. She was just a job to him. He certainly reminded her of that enough times.

"My husband was an undercover narcotics agent. I wonder if they ever crossed paths."

13

Trey opened the door to the Suburban, needing a little space from Renner's venting. He didn't get it. Renner slid in the other side and continued his tirade.

The train arrived five minutes ago. Which meant Jake had a five minute head start on them. He could be anywhere.

Trey glanced at his watch. Forty-five minutes before the funeral.

"The train's the only way he could have gotten here on time. I suppose he could have thumbed a ride, but that's pretty dicey." Trey cut Renner off.

Renner pinched the bridge of his nose. "Yeah. The kid made it all the way to Chelsea's the first time, and I'm sure he's got what it takes to find his way back. He's probably well on his way to the funeral." Renner closed his eyes and shook his head. "It'll be desk work for me from now on. Hamilton's going to have a fit."

Trey started the engine and entered the address of the funeral home into the portable global positioning system. "Let's stop thinking about Hamilton. You were protecting Jake from his father and his cronies. Not Jake from himself. Now, focus."

"Yeah. You're right. I wasn't really expecting the kid to take off. We were having a good time together."

"Jake's a good kid. Chelsea says he just wants to say goodbye to his mama. We can understand that."

Trey grinned, thinking about the bag in the back seat. The GPS called out the first instruction.

"Yeah." Renner rubbed the stubble growing on his chin. "I suppose I'd want to be at my mom's funeral, too."

"OK, then. Let's get over there." Trey backed the truck out and turned left, following the GPS's verbal coordinates.

Renner grinned at him. "Let's go kick some butt."

"Let's not. Let's find Jake and get him out of there before anything terrible happens. I have to answer to Chelsea."

Renner twisted in his seat. "Chelsea's here?"

"Yeah. She bullied me into bringing her."

Renner shook his head slowly. "I bet she didn't have to bully too hard. Where is she?"

"At my sister's for now." The GPS called out another turn.

"I see."

"You see what exactly?"

"The handwriting on the wall."

Trey lifted his brows and navigated the turn. "And that would be?"

"Two things. The first option is that we'll both be doing desk work when Hamilton finds out you brought Chelsea along."

Trey grimaced. He'd thought about that. For about two seconds. But then decided he'd rather deal with Hamilton's wrath than Chelsea's disappointment.

"But I think the alternative is more likely. I'm going to need a new partner before too long."

"What makes you think that?" Trey snorted, glancing at his watch. Thirty minutes until fireworks.

He gunned it around the corner, and Renner

grabbed the handle above the seat. "You'll take that desk job to keep her happy. You're not pulling anything on me."

He ignored Renner. "It's show time. Here's the parking lot. Let's take a look." Trey slowed down and practically crawled past the funeral home's parking lot. "See anybody you recognize?"

Renner plastered his shades against the window. "Not yet. Let's drive around the block, see if we can spot Jake sneaking around. But I think we're going to have to park somewhere and do a little foot reconnaissance."

"Yeah. I was afraid of that."

"Getting a little soft in your old age?"

Trey whipped around the block and parked. "Nah. I just don't want anything to happen to Jake. I want Carpocelli right where he is for a long time. Long enough that I don't have to worry about him anymore. It wouldn't break my heart for him to be old and using a cane before he gets out."

Renner opened his door and chuckled. "You may be old and using a cane before this is all over. But I can't say that I blame you."

"Ready?" Trey exited the truck.

"Yeah. What's the plan?"

"Find Jake. Get out. Easy as that."

"Your wish is my command. Let's go, buddy."

❧❦

"He's not here," Trey whispered, moving close to Renner behind a column in the reception area. They'd searched the entire building, every memorial service in session, every stall in the bathrooms. The men's. And the ladies'.

With the exception of one room.

"He's got to be here." Renner rubbed his chin. "Where else can he be?"

"Think, Renner. Where would a fifteen year old hide?"

Renner stalled. "You don't think..."

"Maybe." He didn't like the idea, but he wouldn't put it past the kid. If he wanted to be here, he'd find a way. "Let's go check."

They ducked into the darkened storage room. Caskets were stacked everywhere.

Renner locked the door and turned around with a groan. "Not quite what I signed up for when I took this job." He raised his voice. "Jake, if you're in here, you might as well stay put."

"Would you be quiet? Do you want to bring everybody running?" Trey scowled at his partner. "Let's get started. You go that way."

Trey opened the first casket lid. No bodies. Relief exploded in his chest. He swiped at the sweat on his forehead.

He opened another. No bodies.

Renner popped open one coffin after another. Nothing.

Whispered voices carried from the hall outside the storage room. He glanced at Renner. Renner raised his eyebrows, questioning.

Trey dipped his head at the casket directly in front of him.

Renner scrunched his face and his jaw went slack. He mouthed, "Are you kidding me?"

Trey shrugged. What choice did they have? They didn't have time to find another place to hide.

Trey lifted the lid of the casket. He lifted one leg, preparing to hop in, and jerked back as a pale face with wide eyes stared up at him.

"What—?"

14

"Busted." The squeaky voice echoed up from the casket.

"Jake, you are going to wish—" Trey's voice boomed throughout the room, a bit louder than he'd intended.

The whispering paused in the hallway. The door handle rattled.

Trey didn't move, didn't breathe. Renner stood frozen with one hand holding a casket lid open, his leg lifted in mid-air.

Trey eased his hand towards the gun he'd tucked away, the coldness of the metal wreaking havoc with his nerves. He slid it out and aimed the barrel towards the door.

He didn't want to shoot anybody in front of Jake. The poor kid had witnessed enough violence for a lifetime. But Trey would do what he had to do to protect Jake.

Nobody moved. *God, let them move on to another room.*

Footsteps echoed down the hallway. Jake started to hoist himself out of the casket, but Trey held up his hand, palm out. Then he put his finger to his lips.

Jake nodded, understanding Trey's silent message, and eased himself back down.

Trey glanced at his watch. One minute passed,

then two. They had to get moving to activate Chelsea's plan.

"Let's go," Trey whispered, holding out a hand to help Jake from the confines of the casket.

Jake stepped out and Trey reached for Chelsea's bag. "Jake, how attached are you to your hair?"

"Huh?" Jake's bushy eyebrows scrunched together.

"And your eyebrows?" They'd have to take care of them, too.

Renner grinned.

Trey couldn't take the credit. "Chelsea's idea. Renner, find a closet where we can shave his head without attracting any more attention."

Jake gasped and automatically reached to pat the top of his head. Trey held up the bag of goodies. "Chelsea wanted you to be able to say goodbye to your mama. Do you have a better plan?"

"Uh, I was just going to sneak into the back after the service started." Even Jake's whisper squeaked.

Trey nodded. He'd have to teach the kid a few things. Things like looking at all your options, planning...Huh? He'd have to teach the kid? *Save it for later, bud, you've got work to do.* "You can thank Chelsea for this later. Unless, of course, it doesn't work."

Renner motioned for them. Trey gave Jake a slight shove on the shoulder. "Let's go, pal. We've got fifteen minutes for this extreme makeover."

"But—" Jake slid his hand across his head.

"This is the only way, Jake." Trey arched an eyebrow, waiting.

Jake sighed, resignation winning the battle. "OK. But can we at least cut it with a number two clip?"

❧

Trey's forefinger gently pushed Chelsea's jaw upwards. After he picked her up from Peyton's, he'd brought her to the marshal's office.

"I take it we did OK?" Trey grinned at her open-mouthed stare.

"OK?" She returned his grin, and then glanced back at the teenager waiting next to Renner in the tiny reception area. "I don't recognize him."

Brick red spiked hair with matching eyebrows, small black-rimmed eyeglasses, and a fake pierced earring transformed Jake into a punked-out teen. Good thing the hair color she'd provided would wash out. But the buzz cut...that was a different story.

Just then Jake turned and saw her. She rushed forward and pulled him into a hug. "Hey, sweetie."

"Hi, Chelsea."

She savored the hug for a moment and then swatted him playfully on the arm. "Don't you ever do that again, Jake Carpocelli. You gave all of us a scare."

"I know. I'm sorry."

"Did you tell these guys you're sorry?" Chelsea tilted her head towards Renner and Trey. "They risked their lives to save yours."

"Yeah."

Yeah. You just remember that, Chelsea. Trey risks his life on a daily basis.

When Jake's eyes moistened, she softened. Poor kid. She looked to Trey. "Did you guys run into any trouble?"

"Trouble?" Trey snorted. "Nah."

Renner chuckled. "Not unless you call hiding in caskets trouble."

Chelsea sucked in a huge breath, and then coughed. "What?" She covered her mouth with a shaky hand.

Trey grinned. "There weren't any bodies in them."

"Well, that's a relief." She exhaled, releasing pent up breath.

"Except for one."

"One?" This was getting worse by the moment.

"Yeah. Jake's." Renner spit the words out between bursts of laughter, slapping Jake on the back. "Quite ingenious. You should have seen the look on Trey's face when he opened that casket."

She turned incredulous eyes to Jake. "You hid in a casket?"

Jake hung his head and closed his eyes.

Trey slung an arm around Jake's shoulders. "It's OK, buddy. No harm done. Just don't go taking off like that again."

Jake raised tortured eyes. "I just wanted to go to my mom's funeral."

Chelsea nodded and turned towards Trey. "I'd like to talk to Jake alone. Would you gentlemen mind giving us a few moments of privacy?"

࿐

"Thanks for going easy on Jake." Chelsea's soft voice soothed his battered nerves. "But I think you're really a softie under all that exterior gruffness."

"Oh, yeah?" He turned to glare, but the slight rise he felt tugging at the corners of his lips must have given him away.

"Yeah." She smiled back, a teasing glint in her gaze. "Softie."

"Don't let Hamilton know that. He already gives me enough grief."

"Oh, I'll keep your secret, Marshal." She turned and looked out the passenger window. The street sign for his sister's house whizzed by. "Where are we going?"

"Do you mind tagging along with me while I check on my Mom?" He glanced at her before navigating a right turn, hope churning in his chest. He wanted her with him.

"Gum on a hot pavement, remember?"

He grinned. "Thanks. But I believe you were referring to our trip to the grocery store when you mentioned the gum."

"It still applies. What's your mom's name?"

"Alice Colten." Trey whipped the truck into a gated community and reached for his wallet to pull out the gate cardkey. He held it against the card scanner and waited for the gate to open.

"Peyton told me she's had MS for about ten years. That has to be tough."

Trey shrugged and drove the truck through the opening. "It's part of life. She's accepted it and moved on."

"Will your dad be home?"

He should have been expecting that question, but it still hit him like a free-falling piano. "My father hasn't been home since I was ten."

Her open lips formed a circle before closing. Chelsea pulled off her ring, and then put it back on. "I'm sorry. I really didn't mean to pry."

He pulled into his driveway and turned the truck off, turning in the seat to face her pained gaze. He tugged her left hand into his. Instead of stilling her nervous habit, his nerves ratcheted up a notch. He wanted to kiss her.

He needed space. Time. And more than anything, a chat with God. "It's OK, Chelsea. No worries."

He dropped her hand, the scorch stinging his hand from where he'd held hers.

15

"Did you miss me?" Trey teased.

Chelsea dried the last pan and opened the cabinet door in Peyton's kitchen, hoping to hide the splotches she felt wandering up her neck.

That was a loaded question.

Did she squirm every time their hands touched while they worked on the dishes together? Did every inch of her body tingle at his nearness? Did she think of him every other moment during the day?

Did she miss him while he helped Renner settle Jake into the safe house late this afternoon?

Uh, yeah.

Coffee! That's what she needed. She suffered from a severe case of caffeine deficiency. She hung the dishtowel on the rack and scooted to the pantry. Away from him, away from the emotions he invoked in her. She felt like a quivering paper clip getting sucked closer and closer to a magnet.

He grinned at her retreat and continued rinsing out the sink. Did he know the effect he had on her?

"Did you get Jake all settled?"

Trey nodded, his blue eyes crinkling at the corners, and his mouth curling in a smile. "Yep. You can rest assured. Renner has him tucked in for the night with a movie, popcorn and sodas." He dried his hands on the towel before sitting down on the barstool.

Trey was a big help in the kitchen. Not only in hers, but his sister's as well. A good man. A keeper. For somebody. "So how long does it look like we'll be in Raleigh?"

He gave her that lopsided grin of his. "We just got here today. Don't tell me you're ready to get back already?"

She shook her head. "No, that's not it. I was just wondering what day I should plan on going over to visit my family. Aha." She held up a coffee filter in victory. "Would you like some coffee?"

Trey groaned. "I'd love some. That is, if you think you can find some in my sister's well-organized kitchen?"

Chelsea smiled. She buried her head deep in the pantry and scanned the shelves. She held up the can of coffee. "Got it."

She poured water in the decanter and pushed the brew button. Instantly, the aroma of brewing coffee saturated the kitchen.

"Thank you. Just what I needed," Trey said after she placed a cup in front of him.

Chelsea sat down at the counter and sighed, weariness from the events of the last few days catching up with her. She sniffed the air above her coffee cup, inhaling the rich scent, hoping it would invigorate her. "Me, too."

She brought the mug to her lips and caught the delicate aroma of baby shampoo lingering on her hands. She smiled, remembering the fun she had bathing the two little munchkins. "You have a way with your nephews. They obviously adore you. Thanks for letting me help with them."

Trey had finally convinced Peyton and Grant to

see a late movie while they watched the kids. On second thought, Trey didn't really watch the kids. He wrestled and played with them until they drooped from sheer exhaustion.

Trey turned sideways, his knee gently caressing her leg with the lightest of pressure. She took a deep breath. Maybe she shouldn't have sat at the bar. She'd wait a minute and move to the other side of the counter. Where it was safer. Could he see her heart thumping? Hear her pulse pounding?

He didn't seem to notice her nerves. On the other hand, she could feel every last one of them. Especially when his eyes deepened to the color of the ocean with darkened skies overhead. "I should be thanking you for your help. Especially for the bathing part. I like to play and horse around with them, but when it comes to their baths, I'm scared their little wet bodies will wiggle right out of my arms."

Chelsea chuckled. That had crossed her mind, too. "They are livewires. Just like they should be at this age."

Trey nodded. "Peyton doesn't get out much. She's with them all day long, twenty four seven. Grant would like to take her out more often but she refuses to leave the boys."

"Do you have any other family members around to help?"

He shook his head. "Nah. Just my mom. She plays with them when she's able but she can't watch them by herself." Trey took a sip of the hot coffee. "Mmm. This hits the spot."

Chelsea sipped her coffee, mulling over what she'd learned about Trey today. His dad abandoned the family, leaving ten-year-old Trey feeling like he had to step up to be man of the family. His mom developed MS ten years ago and was now confined to a wheelchair most of the time.

Definitely explained Trey's desire to protect the weak and his continual quest for justice. His job.

"When did you want to visit your family?"

She shook her head. "I'm not sure. I thought I would surprise them. Since I didn't know what to tell them, I didn't call. They'll be pleasantly surprised, I'm sure."

Trey smiled. "Or you'll be unpleasantly surprised if they chose this week to be out of town."

Chelsea frowned and stared at her coffee mug. "I don't suppose there would be much I could do about that."

"Then, I guess you'd have to spend more time with me."

Chelsea's head flew up. Why did Trey's eyes have to crinkle at the corners when he smiled? And why did he have to catch her staring at him tonight, unable to peel her gaze away from his taut arm muscles while he played with his nephews? His gentleness with Jake earlier, and then tonight with his nephews, tugged on her heart.

Was she being unfaithful to Doug's memory? She didn't think so. After three exceptionally long years, Doug would want her to get on with her life.

But Trey loved someone else.

She stifled a groan and stood up from the barstool, almost knocking it backwards. She rinsed out the cup and placed it in the dishwasher, trying to keep occupied before she fell apart. This late night chat was more than she could bear right now.

She was lonely; he was extremely attractive and

attentive. And worse than that, she was afraid. Afraid that she was falling in love with someone who would absolutely rip her heart out. Hadn't she told herself after Doug's death that she would never fall in love with a cop again?

Too many secrets.

Too much pain.

She closed the dishwasher and turned around. "Whoa. Didn't I tell you that you shouldn't sneak up on a girl like that?"

He stood in front of her with both arms touching either side of the counter, all six foot two of him effectively blocking her exit. No escape.

She stared at his broad chest. If she thought her heart was beating loudly before, it was taking off at rocket speed now.

He'd taken his tie off and loosened his shirt collar. She fisted both hands at her sides to stifle the urge to wind arms around his neck or run fingers through his hair.

She could feel her heart beating out of her chest. Surely he could hear it? But as much as she wanted to, she couldn't drag her gaze away from his face, mere inches from her own.

Steely blue eyes searched for something. What, she didn't know. She only knew this time he was going to kiss her.

She closed her eyes and waited, holding her breath. She didn't have to wait long.

His lips brushed against hers, gently at first. Soft. Caressing. Teasing. She responded, molding her body to his. She heard his soft moan, felt his arms tighten around her waist. She lost herself in his kiss, winding arms around his neck, totally and completely absorbed in his embrace, in this man.

He pulled away, dragging both her wrists down to her sides.

What? Her eyes still closed, she groaned and struggled to loosen her wrists.

He buried his face against her neck. "Oh, dear God. What have I done?"

She heard the anguished whisper close to her ear. Chelsea's eyes shot wide open. *Something he didn't want to do?*

"Chelsea. I'm so sorry. I didn't mean for that to happen." Pain oozed from his words.

How could he have not meant for that kiss to happen? Didn't it rock his world as much as hers? *Oh, dear God. What have I done?*

He moved his face away from her neck, his breath coming in ragged gasps. "Chelsea. I have to tell you something..."

One step back. Two more and she could be free from the embarrassment coursing through her body. Well, not exactly. That would probably take awhile. At least she'd escape Trey. She could get away before he tried to soften the blow with placating words. Words that wouldn't say what she wanted.

She lowered her head, closing eyes to shield her pain from him. Whatever he had to say could wait until she was no longer mortified at her response to the kiss.

Which would be...?

Forever?

She tried to pull back, but Trey still trapped her wrists. She tugged again, but he wouldn't let go. She whimpered, opened her eyes to find sunken, hollowed eyes beseeching hers. What did he want from her?

Whatever it was, she couldn't give it to him.

How stupid could she be? Hadn't Trey admitted that he loved someone else? Here he was, probably only trying to give her what amounted to a thankful peck on the cheek for helping with his nephews, and she had blown it totally out of proportion by kissing him back. She had made a terrible fool of herself by letting him know her feelings. Worse, she didn't know what feelings she had for him.

He released her wrists. "Chelsea. Please sit down. I owe you an explanation."

"For the kiss?" She scoffed to keep the tears from bursting, the humiliation from burning in her chest, but remained standing. "Thanks for the offer, but I'd rather not hear it right now."

"No. Not for the kiss. As much as I shouldn't have kissed you, I wouldn't take it back. I'd do it again. And again."

His soft-spoken words got her attention. "An explanation for what, then?"

"For Doug."

An explanation for Doug? Goose bumps popped up on her arms, and her heart plummeted to her knees. What did he know about Doug?

He took a deep breath, swallowed. "I was there when Doug was killed. I need to tell you what happened."

The ticking of the kitchen clock became a pounding hammer, relentless and unforgiving, and the twins' sleepy murmurs over the intercom sounded like gigantic waves crashing against the shore. Chelsea's knees buckled. She sank down on the barstool. It was her turn to take a deep breath.

Relax. Breathe in. Breathe out. She fought for

control of the spinning room, for the nausea that threatened to overwhelm her. *God help me here. This is my chance for answers. Don't let me blow it by not focusing on what Trey has to say.*

He moved to sit beside her and reached for her hands, holding one in each of his. "Chelsea, if I could change anything about my life, it would be that one night. For three years now, it's haunted me. The choices I made, what I did, and even more, what I didn't do."

Chelsea looked up to see his haunted gaze filled with moisture, with regret.

Haunted gaze, haunted gaze. A vague recollection passed through her consciousness. "You're the man I've seen at Doug's graveside every year."

He nodded.

She gulped back the lump in her throat and motioned for him to continue.

"We were taking Carpocelli down that night. We spent years gathering enough evidence to make sure he stayed locked up for good. We knew his habits, where he shopped, what nights he went out, who he hung out with. Everything. Even down to the fact that he always bought flowers for his wife the day after he cheated on her." He stopped when Chelsea gasped, and his hands tightened around hers. "We knew he would be at the florist shop. And what time. We couldn't have asked for a better opportunity. He must have sniffed us out. He walked out in front of Doug…"

"Doug was at the florist's shop?" The official line she'd been told was that he'd been at the pool hall next door to the florist, where he hung out sometimes when he was working undercover. But he wasn't working.

"Yes. He had a bouquet of roses in his hand."

Chelsea's shoulders slumped with relief in the knowledge of her husband's love and faithfulness. She had trusted Doug when others questioned his integrity, and she was glad now that she did.

"I was the agent in charge, Chelsea. I gave the green light to go. When they shouted at Carpocelli to stop, Doug walked out, and Carpocelli grabbed him to his chest and started shooting."

Trey choked, a strangling sound. He cleared his throat. "Our guys returned fire. I didn't call off the operation because we might not have had another opportunity to put this thug out of service. He's killed so many innocent people; not only with the gun but also with the drugs he ships. We had to get him off the streets. I'm so sorry, Chelsea. It's my fault Doug is dead."

"He must have known about the baby..." A sob escaped before Chelsea could restrain it.

"Did you say baby?" Trey's words, barely above a whisper, tore at her heart and split apart old wounds. Wounds that had just begun to heal after three years.

"Two weeks after Doug was killed, I lost our baby. The stress of everything..." her voice faltered. "I had just found out I was pregnant. He must have known, somehow. Can you excuse me for a minute?"

Chelsea tugged her hands away and dashed to the bathroom, splashing cool water against her hot face and praying for relief. She couldn't bear this news, not now. Maybe not ever. All this time she'd prayed to find the truth. Now God was answering her prayers, but she didn't want to hear it. Not like this.

Not from Trey.

She slumped to the floor against the door, bargaining with God. She'd forgo the truth if her life could go back to the way it was a few weeks ago. Before she'd signed the papers to be a teen shelter. Before Jake. Before Trey.

She sat there for what seemed an eternity, the tears spent, but the pain and anguish still warring inside of her. What should she do? Where could she go? Why did God bring Trey into her life to cause this kind of pain? Who was Trey, really?

"Hello. Is anybody still up? We're home." Peyton's cheery voice called from the front door.

Chelsea lumbered to her feet, splashed more water on her face and left the bathroom. She lowered her head so Peyton and Grant wouldn't see her puffy red face.

"G'night," she mumbled, stopping to give Peyton a quick hug. "Thanks for everything."

"Good night, Chelsea. Hope the boys weren't too much trouble?"

Shaking her head consumed what strength she had left. She made it to the guest room door, but not before she saw Peyton marching towards the kitchen, shoulders squared for battle. "What did you do to Chelsea?" a hushed voice demanded. "She's been crying!"

Chelsea didn't wait to hear Trey's response. She closed the door, locked it, and flung herself on the bed.

God, didn't You promise that You wouldn't give us more than we could bear? I'm there, God, I'm there.

16

Hamilton wasn't happy. First, Jake took off. Now, Chelsea. Trey's ear still burned from his earlier tirade. Didn't seem like Trey could ever make the man happy.

Hamilton suggested letting Chelsea go. They had Jake covered. If she wanted to go off unprotected, let her.

Trey disagreed. Which didn't bode well for his relationship with his boss.

They'd settled for a compromise. Again.

He could hang out with Chelsea. Protect her. Unofficially. But on his own time.

Unfortunately, after his mom's bout in the hospital last month, he had only one day of vacation time left. So where did that leave him?

Reporting to the safe house tomorrow.

Taking care of Chelsea today. He couldn't leave her alone after what he told her last night.

He stalked up and down the street in front of the house where he was fairly certain he would find Chelsea and adjusted his tie for the fifteenth time. Three hours after she left his sister's house and fifteen times walking up and down this street, and he was still upset.

Upset? That wasn't the right word.

When he saw her empty bed, his heart had lurched all the way down to his toes. Worse than that stupid ride at the fair.

Scared out of his mind. That's what he was. Until he read her note. Saw that she had taken off on her own.

OK, maybe he was a little aggravated. Hadn't she told him time and again she didn't want his protection? Didn't need it?

Renner got his goat occasionally, but he was just a minor aggravation. This wasn't minor.

This was torture to the nth degree.

He knew why she fled. He'd rocked her world, shattered her perception of him. But she didn't realize what they were up against.

He marched once more past the house and cast a sideways frown at the front door. This was the last time. He wasn't making one more pass. If he hadn't cooled off by now, he wasn't going to. He didn't think he'd be in a better frame of mind by tomorrow at this time.

He should have quit when the chief handed out this assignment. Right there in his office. On the spot.

He couldn't do this anymore. Not after last night. Not after spending time with her last week. Not after the last three years seeing the gentle way she took care of her in-laws. How she cared for teenagers, like Jake, who had no one to care for them. How she took in injured animals because she couldn't bear for them to hurt. How she carefully bathed the twins. He saw the look of yearning on her face...

The whole situation made him feel part of a real family. Made him feel as if he were missing something important in his life.

A special something God wanted for him.

Chelsea.

Why had he blown it by kissing her? Not that he would take back any part of that kiss. Not for anything. He'd enjoyed every second. Until he realized what he was doing. Or rather, what he should be doing. Which was telling her the truth.

But she didn't know what was going through his head. Or his heart. He'd only had time to relay the facts before his sister came home.

He couldn't blame her for taking off. He deserved much worse.

Maybe he should listen to the chief. Wouldn't that be the best way to handle this situation with his boss?

Is that what God wanted him to do?

He stopped his pacing. Looked again at the front door. Trey adjusted his tie again, lifted his face to the sun and looked to God for guidance.

He wanted to protect her. To take care of her. To cherish her. To grow old with her.

He wanted the chance. If she'd give it to him.

He marched towards the front door and rang the bell.

❧

"I know, Dad, it sounds strange. What can I tell you?" Chelsea raised both her hands, palms up. Her mother set a plate of scrambled eggs, orange slices and toast in front of her on the patio table.

Chelsea flashed her mom a weak smile. "Thanks, Mom."

She hadn't thought about the complications of explaining her visit to her parents. Somehow, even with all her explaining, they were under the impression that Trey was holding her against her will.

Maybe he was. At least her heart, anyway.

She'd wrestled with the sheets and the pillows for most of the night, and at four a.m. finally surrendered and got up. But pacing Peyton's guest bedroom didn't work either. She couldn't stay in the house. So, she showered, dressed, and wrote notes to Trey and Peyton. Peyton's was a sincere thank you while Trey's was a terse note telling him where she would be until it was time to go back to Journey's End. She had left the house before anyone was up.

She glanced at her watch and saw that it was well after eight. Trey was probably up by now. She shuddered to think how mad he would be about her leaving, especially right under his nose. But she couldn't bear to stay there today, to answer Peyton's pointed questions. To face him.

No. She couldn't let him see how he'd rocked her fragile world. She'd take on Jake's father single-handedly before she'd be caught in that situation again.

She could blame her sleepless night on the coffee, but she knew that wasn't the real culprit. Every time she tried to concentrate on Doug, the only picture her brain displayed was of the tall, ruggedly good-looking marshal with the intense blue eyes and the scar along his jaw line.

The same marshal who killed her husband. Or, at least, accepted responsibility for killing her husband. Even if he hadn't pulled the trigger.

She wanted to forget that part. Rewind the tape. Play it over.

But the kiss? No way could she erase his kiss. Or how his lips felt so right against hers, his arms…

Her father's voice drew her out of self-revulsion.

"What did you say this man's name was?"

"Trey." Her voice squeaked. "Trey Colten. He's a Deputy U.S. Marshal out of Raleigh. His partner's name is Renner, but I can't remember his last name." Now why could she only remember Trey's last name?

"Colten. Hmm. That name sounds familiar." Her father, the cop. Always trying to connect people and names either to perpetrators of crimes or solvers of them.

She nodded. She'd had that same feeling when he stepped out of the Suburban. Now she knew where she'd seen him. Every year at Doug's graveside.

"Do you think Doug might have had dealings with him?"

Chelsea coughed. This was harder than she imagined. She wasn't ready to spill her guts to her parents. She needed time to process everything, sift through what Trey told her. "Hard to say. He used to be in the Drug Trafficking Task Force before he switched to Witness Protection."

Her father looked at her thoughtfully. "You discussed Doug?"

She nodded.

Her father didn't say anything, just sat there with a blank expression. His cop look. She knew where he was going in his thoughts. Pretty odd to be discussing your dead husband with someone you'd just met.

It didn't seem odd when they were sprawled on the great room floor sipping scrumptious hot chocolate that he had made. Nor did it seem odd to see the tenderness radiating from his eyes when she told him her story.

What felt odd was that she couldn't get a concrete picture of Doug's face in her head anymore.

"Maybe I've read his name in the newspaper."

Chelsea shook her head to clear the fuzz that was her brain lately. "Wh...what?"

"I said, maybe I've read his name in the newspaper."

"Yeah. Maybe. But listen. There's no sense dwelling on it. I just want to enjoy the little time I have with you guys. I won't get too many breaks like this." Chelsea didn't want to waste time hedging around Trey. She only had a few hours.

"You're right, Chels." Her mom spoke up. "What would you like—" the doorbell's chime interrupted her—"to do? Hold that thought. I'll be right back." Her mother pushed back her chair.

"No, Mom. I'll get it. You two stay and finish your breakfast." Chelsea rose to answer the door. If she knew Trey, it was probably for her, anyway.

She took a deep breath and opened the front door.

17

"What do you think you're doing?"

Chelsea couldn't look at the hurt in his gaze. Or dwell on the misery she heard in his voice. She could drink a gallon of water to soothe her suddenly parched throat. Pushing back some errant curls from her eyes, she fixed her toughest glare on him and somehow managed to dredge up her strongest voice. "What do you mean, 'what am I doing'?"

"You can't just up and leave without telling me."

She shifted her gaze down from his glower to the distinctive words emblazoned on the right side of his shirt. *Deputy U.S. Marshal.*

"Don't you want protection?"

No.

Yes.

What I need is protection from you. But she couldn't tell him that. She raised her chin. "I told you. I don't need your protection. Especially not now, in Raleigh, and definitely not at my parents' house."

"Chelsea, is everything OK?" Her dad's voice boomed from directly behind her. Where was her sixth sense lately? She hadn't heard or felt his presence until he spoke. She didn't have to turn around to see his facial expression. She knew what it would be like— hard, tough as granite. His bad cop better-not-mess-with-me look. In this case, it was his better-not-mess-with-my-daughter look.

"Sure, Dad." She turned and smiled at him, a mite on the weak side, but still a smile. "Dad, meet Trey Colten."

"Good morning, sir." Trey reached around Chelsea and shook her father's hand.

"Same to you, son. Why don't you come in and join us for a light breakfast?"

Chelsea gasped, her mouth gaping wide at her father. What part of their conversation made him think she wanted to socialize with Trey? Hadn't she come here to get away from him?

"That sounds great, sir. If you only knew how badly my sister cooks. But, if Chelsea's cooking is any indication of your wife's, then light or not, I'm in for a real treat." Trey's lips curved in a smile. He slid past through the open door and winked at her.

Humph! How dare he? Was he trying to butter up her dad? Judging by her dad's wide smile, it appeared to be working.

"Chelsea got her cooking skills from her mother all right. My wife is the best cook..." Her dad's words trailed off as Trey followed him out on the deck, leaving Chelsea standing with the doorknob still in her hand, mouth still open, staring at the space where they disappeared outside. Unbelievable!

She closed the door gently. She wanted to slam it. Loudly. In Trey's face. But that wouldn't be too adult-like, would it? Right now, she felt like a sixteen year old with raging hormones.

And just like a sixteen year old, she popped into the bathroom to check in the mirror, rearranging some wayward curls and splashing cool water on her hot face. With deliberate steps, she made her way to the sundeck and opened the French door, hearing her mother's gentle peal of laughter.

She glared at him. Now he was cozying up to her mother? What was he trying to pull? And more importantly, why? What did he want from her? She couldn't bear to look humiliation in the face today after what happened last night.

Fine. Let him eat his breakfast. But then she'd send him on his way.

She sat in the last open chair at the table, which happened to be right next to Trey.

"Chelsea, I was just telling your parents that I have four tickets to the stock car race tonight at the County Speedway. I'd love it if you and your parents would join me."

Ouch. Her mouth dropped open, and she narrowed her eyes at him. "Don't you have to take care of Jake or something?"

"Jake's taken care of. Remember what my job is?"

Judging by the twinkle sparkling from his eyes and the visible dimples, he seemed to be enjoying himself. Did he think she wouldn't refuse in front of her parents? She didn't know what game he was playing, but her competitive nature said she could play better. A smile tugged at her lips. "What job would that be?"

Trey ignored the question and glanced over at her father. "Has she always been this stubborn?"

Her father threw his head back, roaring with laughter. "That's my girl, all right. Stubborn as the day is long. But I know one thing," he said, sending an amused glance at her mother, "stubborn or not, she won't miss a stock car race given the opportunity."

Chelsea could feel her face and neck flaming. They

were talking about her as if she weren't sitting at the same table.

Trey turned. His eyes held a gentle glint. "Come on, Chelsea. What do you say? I really want you to come. You'll have time to kick back and relax with your parents while we all enjoy the race."

How could she refuse when he asked like that? With soft words and a tender smile that broke through her defenses. Her heart nosedived into the pit of her stomach. She'd be sorry. She just knew it. But she couldn't say no to him anymore than she could stay out of her kitchen.

Excitement overrode fear as she raised her chin, looked him straight in the eye. "I'd be delighted."

❧

"I'm sorry Hamilton pulled me off your case." Trey leaned over, his forearms pressed against the open window of her truck.

"I'm so sorry, Chelsea. It's my fault Doug is dead." The words ricocheted in her head. She got the hidden message.

She opted for a lighter tone, ignoring the innuendo. "About time. Now I can get back to my life."

Adrenaline from the stock car race pumped through her veins like a rocket taking off. It had nothing to do with the fact that Trey's face lingered mere inches from hers. Or how much fun she'd had with him at the race.

At least that's what she told herself.

After his confession, she wasn't ready for anything else. She needed time to digest, time to pray, to think.

"Yeah. You can get back to your life." His sigh,

heavy with remorse, rocked her conscience. He reached into his pocket, pulled out an energy bar and handed it to her.

She tilted her head and held the bar in her hands. "What's this for?"

"For the drive home. I don't want you feeling faint."

She smiled. How sweet of him. "I doubt Journey's End will be quite as exciting without you around."

He laughed. "Let's hope not."

Confusion settled in her chest. "Trey?"

"Yes?"

"Will you be coming back our way? Bringing Jake with you?"

"I can't say right now. We'll keep him safe. You have my word."

He didn't say he would come back. She swallowed the disappointment. What did she want from him?

A kiss. That's what she really wanted.

She leaned closer to him and held her breath, willing him to kiss her. Two inches were all that separated his lips from hers...

Trey exhaled and heaved himself from the open window, regret lingering in his eyes. "Stay safe, Chelsea."

Tears pooled in her eyes, and she swiped them away with her sleeve. She cranked the truck and headed for I-85 south, allowing the tears to stream down her face.

She'd been down this road before.

She'd vowed not to do it again.

18

Trey guided the Suburban around the hairpin turns at a crawl, his knuckles white from gripping the steering wheel, while the power of the storm rocked the huge car back and forth. The wind picked up its intensity, effortlessly whipping around the gigantic treetops, sending debris hurtling through the air.

Why hadn't they checked the weather before they left Raleigh this morning? They had plenty of time while they waited for Jake to finish his meeting with the attorney. Not very smart on their part.

And he sure didn't like the idea that Chelsea might be alone in this.

He smiled. Well, probably not alone. She had Kalyn, Molly, Snuggles, the ducks...

Trey repositioned in the driver's seat, trying to get rid of the damp feeling. He was tired. Drenched to the bone. Ready to get to out of this storm.

When he pulled into the driveway of the safe house, Trey gave a heavy sigh, his stomach rolling after eating that truckload of pancakes earlier. He pulled antacids out and stuffed one in his mouth.

"We're at the safe house, Jake."

"What do you think's going on? It seems worse than a normal storm would be around here." Renner's worried expression matched Jake's.

"Don't know. Why don't we go in and turn on the

TV? Maybe we can catch the weather before the electricity goes out."

They hustled Jake inside. Renner turned the television on while Trey headed outside to bring in the luggage.

The rain attacked him like BB gun pellets. He opened the back, tugged out Jake's backpack and gathered his and Renner's things. He glanced around before making a run for the front door.

Renner opened the door for him. Trey breezed inside, dropped all the bags on the floor and shook his head. Droplets of water flew everywhere.

"Hey!" Renner complained.

"That, partner, is what you call brutal." Trey jerked his head towards the window.

"You know that hurricane that went through Florida?" Renner asked.

Trey nodded, flicking more water from his hair, and Renner continued. "Came right up on its way through Georgia. It's not a hurricane anymore, but we have tropical storm force winds."

"Well, that explains it."

His cell phone vibrated. Trey pulled it out and looked at the caller ID. "Hamilton."

This couldn't be good. The chief almost never called. He connected the call. "Colten. Go ahead, chief."

"Colten, I'm glad I got you. I was worried the storm would knock out cell phone service." No worries there. Trey pulled the phone slightly away from his ear. This job carried enough risks. He didn't need to add deafness to that list.

"I can hear you loud and clear. What's up?"

"You need to head back to the shelter."

੭∼੬

Chelsea turned off the giant television with a flick of the remote. She was in for a long night.

Usually, she loved this time of late afternoon, early evening. Sometimes she'd sit outside on the deck and listen to silence settle like a comfortable blanket, especially after an emotionally charged day counseling her students.

But not tonight. She tossed the remote on the couch and stood up.

She cracked the window open in the great room, watched the breeze pick up the curtains for a few minutes, and then did the same thing with the dining room window. Might as well let the house breathe while she had the chance. She took a deep breath, inhaling the crisp fresh air and caught the scent of pine that gusted through the room.

The gentle breeze swayed the curtains, contradicting the storm raging outside. Huge pine trees looked ready to snap in half, and towering oak canopies whipped around unnaturally. Large-sized limbs fell into the yard like leaves.

Chelsea loved storms. Rain made everything seem so clean and new. Gave everything a fresh start. Washed away all the impurities.

Fresh start. Impurities washed away. *Just like the forgiveness Jesus offers.*

No. She didn't want to think about Trey right now.

How about Kalyn? Her parents had called while Chelsea was in Raleigh and asked Kalyn to come for dinner tonight. Chelsea whispered a prayer for Kalyn's emotional well-being and for reconciliation with her parents.

She sighed. She might as well get something accomplished with her evening. Just in case the power went out, she'd better have her supplies ready. Located so far out from civilization, electricity was always the first to go.

She sauntered into the kitchen and started a fresh pot of coffee brewing. Then she dug through the pantry until she found a flashlight and some candles.

She could get ahead on some baking. Maybe combine ingredients and if the power went out, wait until the power returned to bake them. Yeah. That's what she'd do. A couple of pies would work.

Anything to take her mind off Trey.

Chelsea prepped her cup of coffee and took a huge gulp before rounding up the ingredients she would need for the pies. She turned the radio on and started humming with the music while she mixed. She flicked a little flour on the cutting board, spread the dough out, and started rolling.

What was Trey doing? Would she see him again? Did she want to see him again? When were Trey and Renner bringing Jake back to the safe house? Maybe they weren't bringing him back here. Maybe Hamilton would want Jake to stay in Raleigh.

She frowned as she surveyed her piecrust. Lumpy. Maybe she should have brewed decaf.

She leaned over to put some dirty utensils in the sink, and Snuggles poked his sleepy head out of the utility room. Poor thing. He'd been so quiet she'd forgotten he was even in the house. He probably needed to go outside. Big time.

"Come over here, sweetie."

Snuggles hobbled over, and Chelsea leaned down

to rub his head, listening to the pounding rain from the open window. Should she take him outside in this storm? "Can you wait a second? Let's just wait until the rain…"

Thunder rumbled, and lightning zapped something nearby outside. Probably her electrical panel, she thought, as the electricity flickered on and off, and then off completely.

Snuggles whimpered, and hobbled over to the back door. OK, well, the dog answered that question.

Chelsea groped her way through the darkness to the utility room and hesitated with her hand on the doorknob. Maybe she should get the gun. But it was upstairs, tucked safely into her locked nightstand. She snorted. Trey had made her paranoid about going outside alone in her own backyard.

Well, she was not about to go all the way upstairs for her gun just to take Snuggles out for a nature call in the backyard. Chances were probably greater that lightning would strike her than that someone was actually lurking in the woods behind her house.

Wimp! She jerked the umbrella from the coat rack. She hadn't depended on Doug while they were married. She didn't need a marshal to protect her while she took a walk.

She didn't need a marshal for anything. Especially Trey Colten.

She heard the only corded phone ringing in the office on the main floor. She should answer it, but it was probably Jamee worrying about her. She'd call when she came back in. One look at Snuggles told her he wasn't going to hold it much longer. She tugged a windbreaker on and whistled for Snuggles to follow.

She opened the screen door. Although the rain had

relaxed to a heavy drizzle, lightning popped close by and she jumped, almost dropping the umbrella. She clutched it tighter. This wasn't a good night to be outdoors. "Come on, Snuggles, let's make it quick."

She tripped over a tree root but managed to right herself before falling face down in the mud. Why hadn't she grabbed the flashlight? Too late for that now.

Snuggles, with his snout to the ground, took off limping towards the tree line. After being cooped up in the house, he had something on his mind other than a quick trip outside. "Snuggles, don't go too far, kiddo. I don't have my flashlight. Tonight's not the night to play, sweetie."

Thunder rumbled directly above her while white streaks of lightning popped close by. She dropped the umbrella and watched the wind fling it across the yard. What had she been thinking, with lightning zapping all around? This was crazy.

The wind plastered long wet curls across her face, and she lifted hair away from her cheeks. Water trickled down into her eyes.

She shook her head. They shouldn't be out here. She'd have to put out some newspaper on the utility room floor for Snuggles.

With fingers to her mouth to whistle for Snuggles, she didn't have a chance to react to the painful thump to the back of her head. Tiny white lights flickered in the realm of vision. There was no mistaking the distinct odor from the cigar as she twisted sideways, collapsing in the rain-soaked grass.

"Why? What's going on?" Trey asked, fear clawing at his stomach. He could hear the distracted inflection in the chief's tone, picture the chief leaning back in his chair the way he always did when something was on his mind. Trey popped antacids as his stomach lurched.

"We just got word that Carpocelli escaped from prison today."

"What?" Disbelief set in, followed by numbness. He knew not to trust Carpocelli, should have known he had a plan.

The chief continued. "Yeah. Staged a breakout with a buddy. His cohort is dead, but not before he gave us some useful information. Carpocelli's still on the loose. He's headed your way looking for his son. I've just dispatched additional agents from Charlotte."

"I see." No, he really didn't see. Regret kicked him in the gut. Why hadn't he insisted they protect Chelsea? Brought her to the safe house with them?

Trey pounded his fist against the living room wall and attempted to control his voice. And his emotions. "OK. How do you want us to play this out, chief?"

"Get back to the shelter and protect the widow. Have Renner stay at the safe house and protect the kid. You'll both have reinforcements on the way. I'm working on getting another place ready for all four of you. Wait separately, though, until I give you word."

"All right. I'll leave right now."

"Good. And Colten?"

"Yes, chief?"

"Be careful. Look out for yourself. Don't take any unnecessary chances. Carpocelli will either grab his son or kill him." The chief paused, unusual emotion catching in his voice. "He's out for you, Colten."

Trey nodded even though the chief couldn't see his face over the cell phone. "That's a given."

He knew that would be the case. He'd stepped on Carpocelli's toes too many times. And now they had his son. Funny how Carpocelli didn't scare him. Not like a certain feisty curly-haired female did.

He disconnected the call and returned the cell phone to its carrier on his belt. "I've got to go. Carpocelli's out. Headed this way. You stay here with Jake. Hamilton's got reinforcements on the way. I've got to get to Chelsea. Hamilton thinks he's headed there."

Trey saw the fear radiating from the depths of Jake's eyes. He took hold of Jake's shoulders and looked him straight in the eyes. "Jake, it's going to be OK. We're not going to let anything happen to you."

Jake nodded, gritting his teeth. "You don't know my father. He'll stop at nothing to get me. He'll kill me, too, and Chelsea if he knows she helped me. Just like he did my mother."

"I know your father better than you think. I'm the one who helped build the case to put him where he was, and I'm the one who will get him back there. And you don't know me very well. I'll stop at nothing to keep him from getting you. You have my word." He glanced at his partner. "Our word, right, Renner?"

"Absolutely. You have our promise, Jake. We'll do everything in our power to see to it that your father doesn't touch you. Not one finger. Can't give you our word that we won't touch him, though," Renner added forcefully.

Trey couldn't let anything happen to Jake. Chelsea adored the boy. And if he were to admit it, he'd grown rather attached to Jake himself. The kid wasn't anything like his pre-formed opinions. He definitely didn't take after Carpocelli.

He threw open the front door, raced through the pelting rain, and tugged the car door open. Trey jammed the keys into the ignition and punched Chelsea's phone number in his cell.

"Come on, Chelsea! Answer." He tossed the cell phone against the console when she didn't respond.

The fierce winds had abated for now. Occasionally, a gust would practically blow the Suburban off the road but at least it wasn't constant force. Trey used the lull in the weather to try Chelsea's phone number again.

He let it ring a dozen times before disconnecting. Still nothing.

Wait a minute. Her friend, Jamee. Wasn't her husband the fire chief? Either one of them might be able to help. He could call the fire department and track her down that way.

He dialed the office number in Raleigh and had them connect him, frowning as he concentrated on the road. A dispatcher answered the phone on the second ring. "Journey Creek Fire Department."

"Hello. This is Trey Colten, Deputy U.S. Marshal. I'm trying to get in touch with the Fire Chief."

Silence greeted him from the other end of the phone. Trey recognized the problem. "I realize you probably can't give me his phone number but could you call him and give him mine? I need him to call me as soon as possible. It's an emergency."

"Uh, sure. I think I can do that."

"Thanks. Again, it's Trey Colten with the U.S. Marshal's office. Will you be able to call him right now?"

"Sure, but they're out on a call right now. I'll relay the message as soon as I can raise him."

"OK. Thanks." Trey gave the dispatcher his cell phone number before disconnecting.

Thirty seconds later Trey's cell phone vibrated. He snatched it off the console. "Colten."

"Trey. What can I do for you?" Ethan's voice was tight. Trey heard what sounded like a chain saw in the background.

He raised his voice so Ethan could hear him over the commotion on his end. "Ethan, do you know where Chelsea is?"

"No. Jamee talked to her earlier this afternoon, but I don't know where she is now. Why?" Trey held the phone away from his ear at Ethan's loud response.

"Long story, but the short of it is that I'm actually a Deputy U.S. Marshal protecting Jake Carpocelli. Jake showed up at Chelsea's shelter, and we just learned that his father escaped from prison. He's looking for his son. He's not a nice guy on a normal day, but he's probably good and mad right now. He could be heading to Chelsea's."

"Oh, man. That's not good." Dismay colored Ethan's tone.

No, definitely not good. "I haven't been able to reach her by phone, and I'm still a good ten miles away. Is your power out there?" Trey jerked on the steering wheel to avoid a branch whipping across the road.

"Yeah. Our electricity's been out for a couple of hours now. But that doesn't mean Chelsea's is out. Out as far as she is, I'm sure she would be on a different grid."

"Maybe that's why there's no answer at her

place."

"Maybe. Listen. I'm out in this mess. We've had tons of trees down and power lines snapping. I can't break away just now to go out there but I'll radio in and have an officer dispatched out there immediately."

Trey could sense the frustration in Ethan's voice. "Thanks. I should be there within twenty minutes or so."

"Sure. I'll give you a call back once I hear the officer report in."

"Thanks. Stay safe, Ethan."

Ethan let out a tense snort. "Yeah. The same to you."

Trey disconnected his cell phone and laid it on the console, praying that Chelsea was home safe, just without power. They should never have left her alone. What was he thinking? He should have convinced the chief to either let him stay with her or bring her along.

His teeth clenched tight, making his jaw ache with pent-up tension. Two minutes passed, five, ten. How long did it take? He knew the answer. In this storm, it could take twice as long as normal for someone to get to the shelter. No telling how many downed trees they would have to move before they could reach her place.

Or what they would find.

Trey gripped the steering wheel tighter.

Or who.

19

Trey snatched his phone when he heard the vibration as it moved on the console. "Colten."

"Trey. It's Ethan. I just heard back from the deputy who went out to check on Chelsea. She's not there." Ethan's voice appeared calm in the midst of the chaos clouding Trey's thoughts.

Trey winced. Terror squeezed his lungs, gripping so tightly his breath came in short, ragged gasps. Anxiety gnawed away at the lining of his stomach, a little voice inside that kept harping about his inability to help her. To protect her.

He failed again.

"She's not there. She's not there." Ethan's words reverberated in his brain, like a ping-pong ball gone mad.

Oh God, what next? Help me focus on You here, not me and my inabilities and failures. You promised that through You, all things are possible. Please let Chelsea be safe.

"Her truck is there. The deputy is searching the perimeter of her place now, but you know there's a lot of ground to cover."

Was that supposed to make him feel better? He slowed the heavy Suburban down to navigate the next curve. "Ethan, I'm still ten minutes away. My boss has reinforcements on the way. They should be there any time now. Can you let the deputy know?"

"Sure. I'm wrapping things up here, so I'll be heading that way in about five minutes myself."

"Thanks, Ethan. I'll see you in a few."

Ethan's voice echoed in his thoughts as he disconnected the call. *Where is she, God?*

He pushed the button for Renner's cell phone. Renner answered on the first ring. "Any news?"

"I can't get any answer at Chelsea's house. Chelsea's friend, the fire chief, sent a deputy by to check on her, but they haven't been able to find her."

"Any signs of forced entry? Struggle?"

"Ethan didn't say." Trey juggled the phone against his shoulder and reached for his antacids, holding the steering wheel with his other hand.

"Well, it finally stopped raining. She probably just took a walk for some fresh air. Maybe she just needed a breather after being cooped up by the storm all day."

Trey sighed, responsibility weighing heavy on his heart. "Yeah. Maybe."

Jake's pasty white face blasted his consciousness. This had to be tough on the kid. Not only was he terrified, but he probably also felt guilty for potentially bringing harm to Chelsea. The kid loved her. But then, didn't everybody?

"How's Jake holding up?"

"Not so good, but we've been talking."

"Good. I've got to go, buddy, I'm here." Knuckles white from maneuvering the final curve before rounding into the driveway for Journey's End, Trey blew out a long breath and disconnected the cell. Everything would be all right; it had to be. He couldn't be responsible for anything happening to Chelsea, not after all the blame he carried for so many years over Doug's death. He said another silent prayer.

Police cruisers, unmarked cars, and all kinds of fire department apparatus dominated Chelsea's parking lot. Red and blue lights flashed wildly, lighting up the entire yard. Trey jerked the Suburban to a stop.

He sprinted towards a couple of deputies huddled together and flashed his badge. "Excuse me. Have you seen the fire chief? Or the woman who lives here?"

One of the deputies nodded his head in the direction of the barn. "Fire Chief's over there. With the girl."

With the girl? Trey thanked them and bolted to the barn, trying not to let either fear or hope take hold. Inside, he found Ethan talking with one of his firefighters. "Ethan. Where is she? Have they found her?" Fear gripped Trey's heart. He said a silent prayer to trust God and His sovereignty.

Ethan turned a grim face to him. "The deputy found her knocked out at the edge of the property. She has a good-sized goose egg on the back of her head. The paramedics want to take her to the hospital, but she insists she's not going."

Relief coursed through his body. He closed his eyes and allowed his face to relax. "Thank You, God. Where is she?"

Ethan pointed. "Over there."

Trey turned in the direction he pointed. No wonder he hadn't seen her. Three paramedics and a deputy formed a semi-circle around her stretcher, and he could see that she was trying to tell them something with her hands.

Ethan grabbed his arm before he could leave. "We need to talk."

Trey's mouth was suddenly parched, dry, as if a

wad of cotton was stuck in it. Was this the conversation where Ethan told him he did a lousy job of protecting Chelsea? Didn't Ethan think he knew that already? "Sure. After I see Chelsea?"

Ethan nodded.

Trey elbowed his way through the circle surrounding Chelsea. Her auburn curls fanned out against the white sheet, the spattering of freckles accentuating her ivory skin. He caught the tail end of what she was saying to the paramedics. "...not going to the hospital. I'm waiting for somebody."

When she caught sight of him, a crimson color shot up her neck to her face. He loved it when she blushed. Who was she waiting for? Him?

Trey nodded to the paramedics and flashed his badge at the deputy standing over Chelsea. "Can you give us a few minutes? Let me try and talk her into going to the hospital."

Trey waited until they walked away before taking Chelsea's hand, tucking it firmly in his own. He used his other hand to scrape some mud off her cheek. "You can't hide those freckles, you know."

She scoffed. "As if."

"Can you tell me what happened?"

"Snuggles had to take a walk."

"You took Snuggles out in this?"

She shrugged. "What was I supposed to do? The poor dog was cooped up all day."

He nodded, understanding her dilemma, and rubbed her hand with his thumb. He needed the contact to calm his nerves, to tamp down his frustration with his boss. He should have been here with her. "Where is your dog?"

"Kalyn took him inside. Listen, Trey." She tugged

her hands away and levered up from the stretcher. "Somebody hit me from behind. I didn't see it coming. I didn't hear anybody behind me, either. Whoever it was knocked me out cold. Wait until I get my hands on them."

Trey put his hand on her shoulder and gently pushed her back down. "Whoa, sweetheart. You're not going anywhere. Now tell me what happened, starting from the beginning. Don't leave anything out. This may have something to do with Jake's father."

Her green eyes glinted with determination. Trey recalled a phrase his mother used to say about someone looking "spitting mad."

"What do you mean, it might have something to do with Jake's father? Jake wasn't even here at the time. And didn't you say his dad was in prison?"

"Was."

Chelsea's eyes widened.

"Chelsea, Hamilton called me a few minutes ago. Jake's father escaped prison today. I tried to call here but couldn't get any answer."

"But why would he want to hurt me?"

"Maybe we're grasping at straws here. Just tell me what happened," he said softly.

She relayed everything she could remember, even to dropping the umbrella. "The deputy says it looks like a tree limb hit me and knocked me out. But, I know it wasn't a tree limb. I distinctly remember smelling a cigar as I fell."

He shuddered. She went outside armed with only an umbrella to fight off Carpocelli or one of his henchmen? "Why didn't you take your gun with you?"

She snorted and fiddled with her ring. "In my own yard?"

It wasn't her fault that Hamilton pulled him off the case. He took her hand again and linked her fingers through his, brushed silky curls back with his other hand.

He wasn't thinking clearly here. All he could focus on was that she was hurt, and he hadn't protected her.

"I'm sorry that I wasn't here to protect you."

"You were where you should be. Protecting Jake." She pulled her hand away and stilled his hand from brushing her curls. "I don't need your protection." Her voice said one thing, but the sight of her delicate shape on the stretcher told him something different.

She didn't need it? OK, maybe he was the one who needed to protect her. He wanted nothing more than to wrap her in his arms and to make sure nothing could ever hurt her.

Including him.

He was scared out of his mind.

He loved her.

But his love wasn't enough if he couldn't take care of her when she needed him.

Chelsea's green eyes glinted, and she leaned forward slightly resting on her elbows, her pain evident in the lines across her face. "You're looking at a woman who doesn't need or want your help or protection, Deputy U.S. Marshal Colten. My dad was a cop. My brother is a cop. My husband was a cop. They taught me to take care of myself. I'm not about to back down when I feel threatened. And I will not let anybody scare me away from my own property. Got it?"

Ouch! He got it all right. She didn't need him. Or want him.

Trey couldn't let her know how much this episode

scared him. "Let me go talk to the deputy and look around. Will you go to the hospital?"

"No."

He scowled. Not the answer he was hoping for. "Why not? You need to be checked out."

"I'm not going. I'm staying right here. In my house. I told you no one is chasing me out of my own house. Including Jake's father." Her chin was jutting out. Again.

He nodded, strangely encouraged by her ferocity. "OK. I'll be back in a few minutes. You stay right here and try to relax. OK?"

She nodded her head, wincing in pain from the effort. He grabbed her hand again and squeezed it gently before releasing it.

Trey walked over to Ethan. "She doesn't want to go to the hospital. Can your guys give her something for pain?"

"I'm sure they can but I'll double check with the paramedics."

"What happened?"

Ethan shifted his feet. "When Kalyn arrived home, she saw Chelsea's truck, but couldn't find her in the house. She called the police right away. About the same time you called me."

"Good for her. She's probably the one who scared away whoever tried to take Chelsea."

"Maybe. The deputy thought Chelsea got konked on the head by a tree limb."

Trey gritted his teeth. "Chelsea smelled cigar smoke before she fell. She didn't get hit on the head by just a tree limb. Maybe a person wielding a tree limb."

Ethan blew out a breath. "Wow."

"Yeah. I'll be staying here tonight. Plus I'll arrange

for some additional personnel."

Ethan nodded. "That's good."

Trey shook Ethan's hand. "Thanks. I want to have a chat with the deputy."

Trey asked around and finally located the deputy who discovered Chelsea. After introducing himself and flashing his badge, he asked the deputy where they found her.

"Over here. I can show you." He led the way to a spot at the edge of her property bordering the forest. "Found her right here and this huge tree limb was right next to her. Knocked her out cold."

Trey crouched down. "Can I borrow your flashlight?"

"Sure." The deputy handed him a flashlight. Trey shined it all around, noting the appearance of the ground.

"Thanks." Trey said and handed him the flashlight. The deputy walked away.

He punched in Renner's number on his cell. "Renner, we have problems."

20

"The tree branch didn't knock her out. Somebody dragged her here. Look." Trey pointed the flashlight to the ground, illuminating the path where the dragging of Chelsea's limp form had forced leaves and grass out of the way. "Maybe Kalyn's lights or the sirens interrupted Carpocelli or his guy. Who knows? But, the tree branch definitely wasn't the only culprit."

Ethan, and Sage Michaelson, another deputy marshal from the Charlotte office, followed the path with their gazes. Sage agreed. "You're right. Carpocelli or one of his guys has to be around here. Where do you think they were headed?"

Trey grunted. "Don't know. It's kind of hard to tell in the dark, without being able to see the entire property in perspective. Maybe we should come back out at daybreak and check around some more."

"Yeah. Maybe we'll see something that's not obvious tonight." Sage agreed, walking farther ahead on the path.

"What does this mean for Chelsea?" Ethan asked, grim reality evident on his face even in the darkness. "I'd hate to see her run out of her own home because of this. She was so excited about the shelter opening up this summer."

"The shelter will be shut down for awhile. We can't have teens showing up under these circumstances. Chelsea will understand that."

Ethan raised his shoulders, started to speak. "What are you going to do to protect…"

With their track record, Trey could understand Ethan's hesitance. Determination steeled Trey's lips in a firm line. "We'll do everything we can to ensure her safety, Ethan. We're not leaving her here alone."

Ethan looked at him, gaze unwavering. "I'm sure you'll do the best you can to keep her safe."

The best he could?

Trey would give his life to protect Chelsea.

అఄఄ

Chelsea woke to the sun streaming through her bedroom window. What day was it? What time? Why hadn't her alarm sounded?

Her gaze shot to the clock. Nine o'clock! How could she sleep through all that noise? She had to get to school.

She sat up and swung legs over the side of the bed, a hand bolting to her aching head. Suddenly everything spun wildly, and darkness fought for control.

"Oh no, you don't. You're not passing out on me." Trey appeared from nowhere and steadied her back on the bed.

Trey? Ah, blessed summer. No school. "I think I would feel better if my head actually did split in two."

Trey chuckled. "I'm sure. It's time for another pain killer." He grabbed medicine and the cup of water on the nightstand.

"Thanks." Her hand shook as she took the cup and pills.

"I brought you a bagel. You should have something in your stomach when you take that." After she downed the medicine and a swig of water, he handed her the bagel and pulled the chair closer to the bed.

"Did anybody ever tell you that you would have made a great nurse?" She grinned, thinking back to his comments from last night. "Never a paramedic, though. Your stretcher-side manner is deplorable. You would never be able to get away with all the frowning and scolding you did last night."

"Is that right, eh?"

Trey looked at her strangely, a mixture of tenderness and concern glowing from his eyes. The same look he had when he fed Molly. She started. She had to feed Molly. No. The animal rehab company had picked Molly up while she'd been in Raleigh.

Trey was only doing his job. Especially last night. He'd scolded as if she were some goof ball who couldn't take care of herself.

"Chelsea, Hamilton is working on getting a safe house for all of us." Trey's eyes focused on the bedcovering.

"What? No, I'm not going. I told you. I'm not letting somebody run me out of my own home." The bagel stopped halfway to her mouth.

"No arguments. You're not safe here. Obviously."

Chelsea popped the piece of bagel in her mouth, studying Trey's purposely-hardened expression. The lips were set in firm lines. The eyes that brooked no argument. No compromise.

A shirt emblazoned with the words Deputy U.S. Marshal.

࿇

Trey stepped onto the deck, his hairs pricking at his neck, shrieking danger.

Something was wrong. He'd felt it all morning. His sixth sense screamed that someone watched them, using the trees as a cover. Trey lowered his body until he squatted next to the deck railing and squinted his eyes to scan the surroundings.

Not seeing anything out of the ordinary, he willed his body to relax while anxiety chewed on his insides. This "being watched" feeling was probably due to the two undercover agents. Although he'd just checked with them to tell them he was heading outside, he'd check again in a couple minutes.

Trey walked back inside and refilled his coffee mug. Kalyn rinsed her cereal bowl and put it in the dishwasher, frowning when she looked at his face. "Everything OK?"

"I'm not sure."

"What do you mean you're not sure?" Her voice wobbled as she rubbed her belly.

"Something doesn't feel right to me."

She nodded, finished wiping the counters and hung up the towel. "Will you be here all day?"

All day and all night. As long as Chelsea was in danger. "I plan on it. Why?"

"My mom wants to take me shopping for the baby. Will you stay with Chelsea?"

Good. One less person to worry about. "I'm not leaving Chelsea alone, so yeah, feel free to go shopping with your mom."

She nodded and grabbed her purse from the utility room.

"Give me a minute to warn the agents."

"Sure."

Trey unclipped his radio from his belt. "Perimeter One. Are you in place?"

"Ten-four." He could barely make out the muffled response.

"Perimeter Two?"

"Affirmative."

"Kalyn is heading off the property."

"OK."

"Ten-four." Sounded like Perimeter One had a little cold.

"Thanks." Kalyn headed out the door.

Trey picked up his cell phone and pushed Renner's number. "Everything OK over there?"

"Yeah. You?"

"I suppose. I don't like my gut feeling today," Trey whispered, harshness taking over his tone.

"What's the matter?"

"I don't know. I checked outside, can't see anything. Perimeters check out. I just don't like this sitting and waiting."

"Well, at least you're sitting and waiting in the comforts of a home like Chelsea's. This place isn't quite as nice as where you're at."

Trey chuckled. "Sorry. You're right. I can't complain."

"How's Chelsea?"

"Sleeping right now. I'll go in and check on her in a while."

"Tell her Jake's been asking about her. He's really upset about the whole thing."

"I don't think I'll tell her he's upset, but I will tell her that Jake's been asking about her."

"Yeah. Have you heard anything from Hamilton?" Renner asked.

"Not yet."

"Me, either. Guess we just have to wait it out."

"Yeah. Maybe I'll give him a call after I check on Chelsea."

"Let me know what he says."

"See ya."

Trey disconnected the phone and headed towards the bathroom.

❧❧

The lab's nails clicked along with Chelsea's slippers as she padded into the kitchen, disappointment tightening her chest. "Where is Trey, Snuggles?"

He hadn't left her side since last night. Every time she'd peeked through hooded lids, Trey sat in the chair next to her bed, Snuggles laying at his feet. Reading her Bible, reading the newspaper, working the Sudoku puzzles with a frown on his cute face.

Chelsea smiled at the pup's mournful gaze, picked up the coffee decanter and put her hand on the side. Cold.

She needed some caffeine bad. Before she suffered from a major meltdown. And cold coffee didn't work for her.

She turned on the tap water and poured some into the decanter. Then she filled the machine. Scooping some coffee into a filter, she turned to put it into the coffeemaker.

She wrinkled her nose, feeling a sneeze coming. What was that foul odor? Snuggles let out a low growl.

A rough hand clamped around her mouth and nose, cutting off her breath. Cold metal jammed against her neck.

Snuggles barked twice. The man kicked him, slinging him backwards. Snuggles staggered, a deep growl vibrating from his throat.

Was this Carpocelli? The man Trey had warned her about for weeks?

"Don't say a word or I'll kill you like I did your boyfriend." A gravelly voice spit the words near her ear.

Her boyfriend? He killed Trey?

He dragged her out the door.

Be strong and courageous. I will never leave you nor forsake you. God's promise, one that kept her going through the dark days after Doug's death, helped settle her spirit while Carpocelli dragged her to a path behind the barn.

"I'm taking my hand away, but one scream and you're dead."

"Wh-what d-do you want with me?" Hearing the hysteria bubbling through her voice, Chelsea coughed to clear her throat. She'd never been face to face with a cold-blooded murderer.

I will never leave you nor forsake you. Don't show any emotion. Never let them see your fear. God's promise and her father's warnings about abductions mixed together. After every abduction case he worked, he'd drilled those words into her teenage brain.

She couldn't let this freak know how much he frightened her. Without any weapons, she didn't think she wanted to make him angry with her, either. And her self-defense? Forget about it. She hadn't practiced in years.

Yep. She was afraid.

"Just shut up and do as I say." Jake's father growled from behind, pushing her further away from her house, down a path overgrown with trees and bushes.

He forced her to lead the way. Chelsea spotted a good-sized tree limb ahead. If she could let go of the branch at just the right moment so that it slapped him square in the face...

One, she grabbed the branch.

Two, she pushed the branch forward enough to get by.

Three, ducked and let it fling backwards.

She crouched. Heard the *oomph* and knew her target landed. It was now or never.

She sprinted.

He caught her arm before she'd taken four steps and flung her around, landing a wallop to the left side of her face.

Pain exploded in Chelsea's brain, and the world went dark as her body crumpled to the ground.

❧❧

Trey knocked on Chelsea's closed door. No answer.

Maybe she was dressing. He knocked again. No answer.

He turned the doorknob and pushed the door open slowly, not wanting to wake her if she sleeping.

The bedcovers were pulled back, with no sign of Chelsea in the bed. He smiled, knowing she couldn't stay out of that kitchen for long.

His smile faded when he heard Snuggles bark. A frantic, desperate bark, coming from the kitchen. Trey's pulse rate spiked. He took the stairs two at a time.

At the entrance to the kitchen, he jerked to a stop.

The back door was wide open.

Fresh black coffee grounds littered the kitchen floor. His heart plummeted to his knees. What happened here? Did she place the filter down on the counter and the wind picked it up?

Or was she abducted right out from under his nose?

Snuggles limped to him, his growl fading to a whimper. He stroked the dog's head. "Stay," he commanded.

Trey looked outside. Not seeing her anywhere in the back yard, he unclipped his phone. This could not be happening.

"Perimeters One and Two. Do you see Chelsea outside?" Trey tried to keep the fear from taking over his voice. It had already consumed his gut.

"No. Isn't she inside with you?" The first agent responded.

"No. I need help here. *Now!*"

"What's the problem?"

"Chelsea is missing." Trey didn't care if he used her name over the radio. If Carpocelli had snatched her, then he already knew who she was. "I need you both to search the grounds immediately."

He headed outside. "Chelsea!" He yelled into the breeze but his voice floated back to him. "Chelsea!"

No answer. Why hadn't he listened to his gut earlier?

Now what?

The only thing he could do was pray. So he did.

21

Chelsea winced and rubbed the baseball-size lump that was her cheek.

Carpocelli dragged her body over a rough spot on the ground, and she moaned, but kept her eyes tightly closed. Let him believe she was still unconscious. It would give her time to plan her escape. And dragging her weight around would slow him down.

Give Trey more time to find her. She gasped, a sob breaking from her throat. Had he really...

I can do all things through Christ who strengthens me.

Think happy thoughts, she told herself, dwell on pleasant things.

Like the fun she had with Trey and her parents at the car race. How thoughtful he was, feeding her animals and giving her an energy bar for the ride home. Like how right and good it felt to be kissed by Trey.

What did it matter that she didn't want to admit that?

She didn't want to dwell on the other stuff. Not right now. She scowled. Happy, remember?

What did Jake's father want with her anyway? Was he using her to get to Jake? Didn't he know she didn't know where Jake was? Would she be strong enough to withstand whatever torture he dealt her?

Carpocelli stumbled over a branch and tripped,

grabbing her hair to keep her from escaping. She bit back her scream, tasting blood on her bottom lip.

Her heart cried out for Trey. She wanted him here, protecting her. Why had she told him that she didn't want his protection last night?

Had Carpocelli really...

She stopped that train of thought.

Trey would have protected her with his life. She knew it.

This whole ordeal was her fault. Trey had tried to warn her about the danger. She should have listened. Well, actually, she did listen to him.

She just didn't follow his advice.

Didn't let him do his job.

ॐॐ

"Looks like we just found out how Carpocelli snuck in." Trey barked into the radio, racing to where he spotted Agent Lennard flung into the bushes a short distance from the back door.

Trey's momentum forced him to land heavily on the ground. He grabbed Lennard's wrist, checked his pulse. Weak, but at least he still had one. *Thank God.*

"Sage, get on the phone and get Rescue here. Lennard's been stabbed. And if you haven't already, get Hamilton on the horn. We're going to need a ton of backup."

Sweat dripped down Trey's back and saturated his collar. Frustration churned his stomach. Everything in him screamed to search for Chelsea before it was too late, but he wouldn't leave Lennard by himself. The guy had a three-year-old son and another on the way.

He yanked his tie off, using that to apply pressure

on the wound while checking to make sure he hadn't missed anything else. Trey grasped Lennard's hand, forcing a more temperate tone to his voice than what he felt. "Lennard, hang on buddy. Help's on its way. It'll be a few minutes. Can you hang on, buddy?"

The slight movement of Lennard's head and a soft moan convinced Trey that Lennard heard him.

Anger at Carpocelli gnarled his insides.

God, help me to find Chelsea safe and unharmed. And I pray for justice for Carpocelli. Help me put him back where he belongs and for him to stay there. Even if it's the last thing I do on this earth.

Minutes later rescue units, fire trucks, marked and unmarked police cruisers littered the driveway of the shelter. The rescue truck pulled out of the driveway with Lennard. Ethan drove in, lights flashing.

"I heard bits and pieces over the scanner. What happened?" Ethan huffed, running to meet Trey.

Trey moaned, praying for faith to win over the despair drowning his heart. "Chelsea's gone, Ethan."

A dark look shaded Ethan's face. "What do you mean 'gone'?"

"I'm pretty sure Carpocelli has her."

"How? I thought you had guys here? Around-the-clock protection?"

Trey choked and caught his breath. "We do. She'd been sleeping all morning. I left her to get some coffee, check out the house. I had a weird feeling all morning, so I even went out on the deck. Everything checked out OK. I slipped in to use the bathroom. I couldn't have been in there more than a few minutes."

Ethan put a hand on Trey's back and waited for him to catch his breath.

"While I was in the bathroom, she must have

woke and went into the kitchen to make coffee. Carpocelli stabbed Lennard, one of our men, and then snatched her right out of the kitchen." He nodded in the direction of the disappearing Rescue truck.

Ethan's face clouded. "What do we do now? What can I do?"

Trey snorted his frustration, swiped an arm across his forehead. "Carpocelli will be contacting me. He'll have something up his sleeve, I'm sure of it. Meanwhile, we're going to hunt them down until we find them. And Carpocelli better hope I'm feeling generous when that happens."

Trey's heart felt slashed in half as if Carpocelli had taken the knife to him instead of Lennard. Finding Chelsea, safe and unharmed consumed every available inch of lung space he had. But justice for Carpocelli waged a war within him. The man had killed so many. He didn't deserve to be free from prison, terrorizing innocent people, including Chelsea and his own son.

"How many people do you have out searching?" Ethan asked.

"Twenty officers right now, divided up into four grids. You wouldn't happen to have any search and rescue dogs, would you?"

Ethan's face lit up. "We just hired a new firefighter with a search and rescue dog. Would you like me to call her?"

"Yes. Although you need to stress that this guy is dangerous. We'll have her tag with one of our agents for protection."

Ethan walked a distance away to use his radio, and Trey took a breath. A search and rescue dog was a good idea. The best one so far.

He reached for an antacid; his gut literally ached

right now. This situation was all his fault. If he hadn't become so personally involved with Chelsea, so blinded by his feelings for her, this entire scenario could have been prevented. Somehow, Carpocelli had latched on to his feelings.

If anything happened to her, how would he ever be able to forgive himself? Only by God's grace. That's how.

Although he felt a load lift after he confessed everything to Chelsea in Raleigh, he knew he hurt her. She'd been a real trooper at the stock car race in front of her parents, but he could see the strain around her eyes, the way her shoulders drooped, her constant fiddling with her ring.

But she was still talking to him. A little. That was a good sign, right?

He closed his eyes and prayed silently that the God of all creation would help him find Chelsea, to be able, finally, to ask her forgiveness and give her the time she needed to forgive him.

His cell phone vibrated. "Colten."

"Colten, my man. Just the one I wanted to speak to."

"Carpocelli?"

"The one and only."

"What have you done with her?"

Laughter, low and vile, filled his ear. "She's not exactly my cup of tea, Colten, but then I've been in prison a few months now. You figure it out."

Disgust and revulsion filled Trey's gut, the nausea threatening to overwhelm him. "You touch her, Carpocelli, you'll have to answer to me."

More laughter. "Oh, I'm touching her all right, don't you worry, all the way down to those silky auburn curls –"

"I'll kill you."

"I'll be in touch."

Ethan nudged his arm. He hadn't seen or heard him approach. "News?"

"Carpocelli has her."

"Does Carpocelli know his son isn't here?"

"I don't know. But if I know Carpocelli, I'm sure his plan is to use Chelsea as leverage to get Jake back. And whatever else he has in mind." Trey shook his head to clear the thoughts. He knew Carpocelli's plan included getting to him.

And he had just snatched the one person who could do that.

22

The man's feet were definitely as foul as his mouth. And his eyes.

That's the last time she'd ever look at a pair of socks in the same way. She'd never imagined, not even in her wildest dreams, eating a pair of dirty socks. She'd probably never even wear them again.

Carpocelli had crammed his socks so tightly in her mouth that she couldn't scream.

She wiggled her hands back and forth, eventually rubbing raw blisters on the sides of her wrists, trying to loosen the thick cord binding her hands and ankles. There was no way she was going to get these things untied.

She closed her eyes and caught her breath. That was not the power of positive thinking. She had God on her side, remember? *I can do all things through Christ who strengthens me.* From Philippians somewhere, she couldn't remember exactly where at the moment. She'd seared that verse into her memory after Doug's murder, allowing God's word to cloak her like a warm blanket on a cold winter night.

She looked around the floor of the abandoned shed for something to use. Broken glass, wire cutters, anything. She made a mental list of what she saw—a pair of pliers, an empty lantern, live bugs scurrying across the floor. No rodents or spiders. Yet.

She shivered. Nothing that would help. At least, not at the moment.

Carpocelli had left her a few moments ago to make a phone call. What use did he have for her, one slightly overweight school guidance counselor in a remote area north of Charlotte? Why would he snatch her and not take his own son, Jake? This whole thing didn't make sense.

Maybe a kidnap scenario? Couldn't he tell she wasn't made of money? She didn't wear fancy jewelry or designer clothes. Maybe he wanted some type of swap?

Or had he left her here to die? She didn't think so. Not if the wicked gleam in his eyes when he looked her up and down was any indication. He had plans for her. Plans she didn't want any part of.

She had to get out of here. And fast.

Tears streamed down her raw, swollen cheeks unabated while she took stock.

Wounded spirit, but no broken bones. Tied up in a hunting shed with no way of escape. But at least the jerk hadn't carried out his threat.

At least not with her.

What about Trey?

Her body convulsed in shakes beyond her control.

Stop it! she ordered, swiping her sleeve against her cheek. She couldn't just wait for Jake's dad to come back and finish her off or do whatever evil intentions he had.

Tears would get her nowhere, except killed.

She had to think, to concentrate. There had to be a way out of here. She had to come up with a plan to blow this joint. Pronto. Before he came back.

Straining her back against the wall as hard as she

could, she lifted her body a third of the way off the floor before sliding back down to the ground with a loud thump.

She screamed, although it was unheard because of the socks stuffing her mouth. That wouldn't work. She closed her eyes.

God, please help me here. I don't know what to do. Help me, please!

A subtle peace descended over her shoulders and traveled down aching limbs. Her tears stopped and her body relaxed. The shaking subsided.

She glanced around with a clearer focus. A cot sat snug against one wall, a small upper and lower cabinet with a sink leaned against one wall, and a little cook stove completed the fixtures.

Where was she, anyway? Was this place a shed or was it some type of old hunting stopover? Perhaps some vagrant had taken up residence in here.

A tiny flare of hope took root in her chest. If it was a hunting shed, could there be a knife stashed away somewhere?

She pushed against the wall and slid her feet up close to her bruised rump. She took a deep breath and pressed one shoulder against the wall to brace and repeated the process with the other shoulder.

She inched her way up the wall, sweat beading on her back. Halfway up, she stopped to take a breather, being careful not to slide back down.

She was almost there. Her tongue longed to lick her dry lips. She could literally taste her freedom.

She made it. Limping over to the cabinet, she peeked on the top shelf.

A knife!

I can do all things through Christ who strengthens me!

❧❦

Trey disconnected the cell phone and clipped it back on to his belt while he continued pacing on the front porch of Chelsea's place. Hamilton's voice had thundered a couple hundred miles to inflict pain in Trey's ear. Trey could picture the boss as he hung up, reclining all the way back in the leather chair, squashing that tennis ball he used as a stress reliever. How could Trey lose Chelsea from her own house? *Again?*

Trey exhaled loudly. He had no answers.

At least Hamilton had agreed to run down a chopper to help in the search. It was due to arrive within the hour.

The static in the radio interrupted his thoughts. "Mis...to...mand"

Trey walked off the porch, holding the radio up higher in the air for better reception. "Command. Go ahead."

"Call me on my cell, please."

Uh-oh. This could be good or bad. *Please, God, good news?* Funny how after three years of ignoring God, now a minute didn't pass where he wasn't reaching out to Him in prayer.

Maybe not so funny.

He reached for his cell phone again and glanced at the page in his little notebook that he used to record the cell numbers of the various people out searching. With fumbling fingers, he punched in her number.

Missy's handler, Firefighter Rylee, answered on the first ring. "Missy picked up her scent again." The dog had lost Chelsea's scent at the end of an overgrown path that led to a hidden road.

"What's your location?" He balanced the cell phone between his ear and shoulder while he scrambled for a pen to record the grid numbers that she reported. "I'll be in that area in about ten minutes. You keep searching. Great work. Give Missy a treat for me."

He ran inside the house to look at the makeshift map they had blown up and stapled to the wall. After locating the grid where Missy picked up the scent, he snatched the radio from his belt and alerted Ethan and Sage.

He grabbed a backpack and stuffed it with some orange juice and an energy bar for Chelsea, water, and first aid supplies.

Trey drove as far as he could, a little farther down the road from Missy's area, finally parking Chelsea's truck inside some heavy vegetation to hide it from view. He opened the door and climbed out, grabbing the backpack. He'd have to hike the rest of the way.

He locked the truck and shoved the key deep in his pocket, making a mental note of the truck's surroundings in case he had to find it in a hurry. Ethan was right. Not much here but vegetation. Wilderness.

And hopefully, Chelsea.

Pain and fear rippled, squeezing the air from his lungs. Was she hurt? Had Carpocelli harmed her in any way? What did he want with her? Was it to use her to get to Jake? Or him?

Too many questions and not enough answers. But Trey knew if it came down to it, he would offer his own life if it meant Chelsea was able to leave unscathed.

Shock waves cascaded through his body. That's

exactly what Jesus had done for him.

He gave up His life for him. As a sacrifice. Because He loved him.

Trey blinked. He had never experienced this feeling before. In past cases, his job was to protect the witness, but his safety was always foremost in his mind. Always.

Until now. Chelsea's safety was his priority.

Because he loved her.

He stumbled over a tree limb in his realization and caught a branch to keep from tumbling on the ground.

He loved her.

He loved everything about her.

When he found her, he didn't know what he wanted to do first. Kiss her or scold her. He shook his head. That wasn't entirely true. He knew what he wanted to do first.

Absolutely. Unequivocally. Undeniably. He would take her in his arms and hold her for a full ten minutes. Then, kiss her. For even longer.

If she'd let him.

Trey pushed back a tree limb and ventured farther into the woods. The kiss they'd shared at his sister's house had stunned him. Actually, it wasn't the kiss so much as her response. He smiled as he thought about it, and then grimaced. He should never have initiated it. Why hadn't he started by telling her the truth? Before he kissed her?

He could still feel her soft lips, responsive to his. He loved the way her fingers caressed his chest and how she had wrapped her hands around his neck, gently molding her body closer to his.

He shuddered slightly, thinking how close he came to losing any self-control he had left. He didn't want Chelsea that way. He wanted her in spirit and in truth. As in, forever. As in, marriage. Would they have a chance of building something now? Would she ever find it in her heart to forgive him?

Why hadn't he used that opportunity to talk instead of acting on his emotions? Maybe they could have discussed things, he could have begged her forgiveness, and confessed his feelings for her before Peyton got home.

Trey stopped walking to take a swig of water and wipe the sweat from his neck.

He turned to place the water bottle back in the backpack, and his eyes noted an anomaly off to his right. He caught his breath and forced his body into stealth mode, slowly lowering his knees until he blended in with the high grass. No sense in letting Carpocelli know he was here.

His eyes focused on what had caught his attention. A small shed of some sort. Funny, for a shed to be out here in the middle of nowhere. He glanced at his GPS unit to radio his location to Rylee. Forcing his movements to be deliberate and silent, he unclipped his radio and brought it to his mouth.

23

Trey wasn't sure what to expect when the door to the shed flung wide open, but he was certain this wasn't it.

Chelsea, alone and scared, pummeling her fists into his chest. Somehow, he had in his mind that he was more of the knight in shining armor type, not the bad guy she wanted to attack with all her remaining strength.

He grabbed her wrists to fend off the attack and she jerked away in pain. He looked down where he gripped and saw what caused her reaction. Her wrists were raw and bleeding. Trey moaned inwardly and released her arms, but reached around her waist and pulled her close to his chest.

"No." Chelsea struggled against him as he pulled her tighter against his chest. She screamed. With no muffle except for his shirt, her voice carried.

"Shh, Chelsea. Quiet. Do you want Jake's father to hear you?" he whispered right next to her ear.

He saw the recognition dawn as she forced her eyelids open and looked up, felt her arms slide around his waist. He pulled her into his embrace and she snuggled deep into his chest. He sighed, heavy with relief.

"You're not dead," she murmured.

"It wasn't me I was worried about."

Her tear-stained face lifted to his. "But Jake's father said—"

"Shhh. It's OK, sweetheart. Jake's father is the master of lies and deceit. I'm not dead." Thank God she wasn't either. Sweet relief, if only a temporary reprieve. He found her. She wouldn't have to go through this alone. He would protect her. If she would let him.

After a couple of moments, he grasped her upper arms and reluctantly pulled her away, looking down at an adorable dirt-smudged face, auburn curls wrapping around her neck.

❧❧

"Are you OK?" Trey's gaze swept her face. With his thumb, he wiped away stray tears.

She nodded. Her knees buckled like overcooked spaghetti, her heart stopped beating, and her brain became oatmeal.

Trey was alive! She smiled and closed her eyes. His lips found hers, his kiss soft and gentle. Without thinking, she wound her hands around the back of his neck and gently pulled his head closer. Adrenaline from the past few hours rushed through, forcing her kiss to be bolder, more demanding.

What? Again?

Trey pulled back, and her legs wobbled precariously. What was with this man breaking his searing kiss before she was ready?

She sputtered.

"I'll make it up to you, sweetheart."

"Promise?"

"Promise. One long, uninterrupted kiss. If you

want it."

"There's no *if's* there, Marshal. When. And you just remember that."

"Did he hurt you?" His voice sounded ragged next to her ear. He leaned back to look into her eyes, pain pouring from his expression.

She shook her head, thanking God with every breath. "Not that way."

His grip tightened, and he closed his eyes. "Thank God," he whispered against her neck.

"How did you find me?"

"I'll explain everything when we put a little distance between us and Carpocelli. We've got to get you out of here. Are you ready?"

At her nod, he released her, but kept a tender hold of her hand. He poked his head out the door and scanned their surroundings in both directions before leading her out of the shed. "Let's head for the tree line over there," he murmured, pointing north.

Dodging tree limbs, upturned roots, and giant raindrops, they sprinted for what felt like ten minutes. Chelsea tugged on Trey's hand, gasping for air.

"Can we stop for a minute?" She panted, wiping wet curly hair away from her face.

He nodded, but she noticed he wasn't even out of breath. Trey, still clasping her hand tightly, slowed down and led her to sit down on a huge tree limb. He crouched, resting on his heels, while he pulled at the cord attached to her shoe.

"He tied my feet and hands." Chelsea shuddered and rubbed her wrists. Trey finally yanked the cord free. He took the sweater he had brought and wrapped it around her shoulders while the rain continued to fall, although more softly now.

His eyes warmed her with their raw emotion. "I'm sorry, Chelsea, that I wasn't here sooner."

He sat down on the log next to her and put his arm around her shoulder, warming her with a brief hug. "We can't stay here but a minute; only long enough for you to catch your breath. I need to get you as far away from here as possible. He could be out looking for us now."

Trey picked up his radio and turned the volume lower. "Command One to Fire Chief One and Missy One." His voice rumbled just slightly above a whisper. Music to her ears. She wasn't in this alone anymore.

"Fire Chief One here."

"You've got Missy here, too."

"I've found Chelsea. She was being held in an abandoned shed, but she's safe. We're heading back to the base. Cancel the search and get all officers back to the base immediately. Ethan, can you inform Sage to expedite the chopper?"

"This is Sage. I hear you. The chopper's on its way, along with backup. They should be here within fifteen minutes. What are your coordinates so I can get police units started your way?"

Trey pulled the notebook out of his pocket where he recorded the coordinates for the truck and repeated them over the radio. "We're out now. See you in a few."

"Be careful," Sage added. "Any sign of Carp–"

"Negative on that. But we'll be careful," Trey interrupted before clipping his radio back to his belt. He grabbed her hand again. "Are you ready?"

She nodded.

"Let's go then. Let's get you out of here."

Trey took off at a fast clip with her at his side, his

eyes darting one hundred and eighty degrees. Chelsea much preferred traveling this way, rather than being forced here with a pistol in her back. "How much farther to your truck?" She panted.

"You mean your truck?" He cast a sly glance her way.

"My truck?"

"Your truck was officially put into service by the U.S. Marshal's office."

"We aim to please." She huffed, smiling at the thought of the kiss she would collect later.

∂∽∾

Uh-oh. Change of plans.

Trey skidded to an abrupt stop and quickly fell face-down to the ground, yanking Chelsea down with him. He heard her soft moan. He pinched the bridge of his nose with his fingers. How could he have been so stupid?

He turned his face towards Chelsea and got her attention. He pointed to her truck, with four flat tires, and then shook his head while making a chopping motion to his lips. There would be no talking from this point on. She must have realized the significance of her damaged truck because he heard her slight gasp.

Carpocelli had found the truck. Trey shook his head at his own ignorance. Why didn't he think of that before blaring out the coordinates over the radio? Carpocelli could be lurking behind any one of the thousands of trees waiting to ambush them. Trey pulled out his handgun.

He didn't want to risk using his radio again. It was no longer a safe option. Carpocelli could be anywhere watching them, or at least within hearing distance. With gradual movements, he turned his head, hoping to catch a glimpse of anything unusual or any sudden movements. Not seeing anything through the rain besides hundreds of trees and a beat up truck, he turned, facing Chelsea.

Panic had settled in her wide eyes. "It'll be OK," he mouthed.

She nodded.

Still prone on the ground, Trey turned his head slowly in every direction searching for ground cover of some sort. They had to regroup, plan their next step. Ideally, he knew they should wait for the chopper somewhere close by.

But the chopper wouldn't be able to land here. Too many trees, not enough vacant land for the rotors to get through. Maybe that would be the next step— finding a suitable landing spot for the chopper.

He pointed his finger in the direction he wanted Chelsea to follow him and took off crawling at a rapid pace, gun in his hand.

He didn't hear her moving.

He looked back.

She wasn't there.

24

Not again!

He couldn't have lost her again. She was right behind him.

Then he saw her, lying a few yards back. Relief swept through him. Carpocelli hadn't claimed her as his victim again.

But, what was wrong? Had she passed out from exhaustion? Low sugar level?

He inched back and rubbed her shoulder gently. She didn't respond. Sweat trickled down his back, and his throat felt like sandpaper. He tapped her head this time. Still no response. He took her wrist, careful not to touch where the ropes rubbed it raw, and checked her pulse. Pulse was weak, but OK. What was wrong?

Trey studied her. No signs of trauma. He slowly turned her body around, face-up.

She'd passed out.

Leaning close, he whispered in her ear, "Sweetheart. Wake up."

No response. Her breathing appeared to be normal, and he couldn't see any visible wounds or bite marks on her body. Some juice would probably do the trick.

Reaching around, he took off his backpack, pulled out a bottle of juice, and then the energy bar.

The darkness descending cast shadows across the

ground. Although the rain had finally stopped pelting them, they wouldn't be able to stay in the open without shelter or cover.

Where was that chopper? Why was it taking so long?

Trey looked down at Chelsea again. Still no movement, but he could feel her breath on his face as he leaned close to her. He kissed one cheek and caressed the other with his thumb. "Chelsea, honey, wake up." Still her swollen eyelids didn't open.

He opened the bottle of juice and drizzled a little in her open lips.

A twig snapped nearby.

∂∞∽

Trey ducked behind a tree, trying to apply pressure to the bullet wound in his left arm. He clutched the gun in his right hand. Carpocelli had gotten him with that last shot, which had ricocheted right off the tree and into him. He scrunched his eyes against the hot, searing pain burning up and down his arm.

He couldn't think straight. If only he could sit down, catch his breath. Out of the corner of his eye, he caught a glimpse of someone running towards him.

Chelsea.

He gasped, breathed a thank you to God that she was up and running, but it was short lived. Carpocelli aimed his gun in her direction.

"No. Chelsea, get down," Trey screamed, frantically waving his arms. He stepped in the line of fire, shielding her with his body.

Carpocelli fired his gun.

He felt the thud, and then intense pain shooting, exploding up his leg. Mingled with the throbbing from his arm...

Oh, God, no. He couldn't leave Chelsea helpless, alone with this monster.

Trey aimed his gun at Carpocelli and fired. Carpocelli crumpled on the ground for an instant and then scrambled up to limp away in the opposite direction.

Trey looked from Carpocelli, who was shuffling away, to an inert Chelsea. She'd hit the ground hard when he screamed, her head flat against the dirt. Fear stabbed at his gut, the ache from it worse than the pain from his own gunshot wounds. Had she gotten hurt somehow in the crossfire? Hadn't they each only fired one round?

Trey made the conscious choice to let Carpocelli go free and staggered to Chelsea.

25

Trey reached Chelsea and lowered himself to the ground, propping up against a huge oak tree. The sting in his arm seemed trivial compared to the excruciating pain shooting up his leg. He touched her gently on her shoulder. "Sweetheart. It's over. Are you OK?"

Chelsea's eyes opened, and tears slipped down her dirty cheeks. "Is he dead?"

He held out his good arm, inviting her to rest with him against the tree. She sat up and snuggled in the cradle of his arm. He grimaced, not only from the pain, but at the potential consequences of Carpocelli's shot. How close he'd come to losing her before he had a chance to tell her he loved her. "No. He's not dead. Are you hurt anywhere?"

"No, you yelled just in time. Good thing we had a little practice with that stop, drop and roll procedure beforehand." She smiled, but it faded when his blood soaked through her pajama pants from his leg wound. She bolted straight up. "You've been shot."

Sweat beaded down Trey's face as the pain from his wounds began to take hold of his brain, his vision blurring. "I couldn't let him hit you. It's OK. Put your head back here. He's gone for right now. I just want to hold you for a second."

Chelsea leaned back against his shoulder again, and he closed his eyes for an instant, hoping to block out the pain. He sighed and rested his head on hers. Just where he wanted to be.

Actually, the more he thought about it as he drifted off, he would rather be at her house on the porch, rocking in the swing with her snuggling in his arms. Rocking. Rocking.

His last thoughts were of the two of them rocking on the porch swing, watching two little ones play in the yard. With a faint smile on his lips, he allowed his body to succumb to the pain.

❧❦

Chelsea didn't dare move a muscle. Trey had passed out against her head, his uneven breaths blowing curls against her face.

What was she going to do? Trey needed medical attention, fast, and a crazy raving lunatic was still out here.

Where was Trey's gun? She twisted her head to looked around. He still gripped it in his right hand, the one that he had tucked around her waist. She gently took it and grasped it tightly.

If Carpocelli came back, he wouldn't get close enough to either of them to do any harm. She knew how to use a gun. And she would if she had to.

She caught her breath. Trey had called her "sweetheart." He'd taken a bullet for her, risked his own life for hers.

She knew she had forgiven him for his role in Doug's death. Unequivocally, undisputedly, yes. Trey wouldn't have killed an innocent bystander in cold blood. He would have done everything in his power to protect innocent people. Carpocelli was the enemy here.

But, the forgiveness issue aside, could she get past the fact that Trey was a marshal? That meant law enforcement...danger...travel. All the things she despised. She craved security. A home. And she craved a family most of all.

When she gave her love away again, it would be to someone who valued her goals as much as she did.

And that meant someone not in law enforcement. Someone who didn't have thugs like Carpocelli chasing him. Someone who wanted a family.

One out of three didn't cut it.

No, it made no sense to get involved with Trey Colten. She shook her head.

But wasn't it already too late?

She turned to look at him, traced his scar line with her fingers. Wiping the sweat from his face with her sleeve, she remembered the gentle way he played with his nephews and the love in his face when he teased his sister. She pictured the excitement on his face at the stock car race, the tender look in his eyes when he spoke with his mother. The pain mingled with love she saw in his eyes when he looked at her. This gentle man had suffered with the guilt of Doug's death for far too long.

Oh yeah. It was too late. Her heart already belonged to him.

The rotors a helicopter's blades sounded overhead, startling Chelsea. Scrambling to get up from her nesting spot next to Trey, she threw the gun on the ground and started waving her arms wildly in the air. "We're here. Here."

The helicopter continued on its northerly path, not acknowledging her presence. She looked down at her green pajamas and snorted her frustration. She probably blended right in with all the trees.

Wait a minute. Where was Trey's radio? She could use it to contact the helicopter, couldn't she? Trey hadn't wanted to use it anymore because he thought Jake's dad had a radio set at their frequency. But he was gone and the helicopter was here. Close by, anyway.

She reached her arms around Trey's waist to where he usually hooked his radio and phone.

That was when she felt blood on his arm. She tugged on his arm and saw the hole from the other gunshot wound. He'd been shot in the leg and the arm?

Oh God, help him. Tears cascaded down both cheeks unchecked. She had to get the helicopter back. He'd never have a chance of surviving if she didn't.

She had to hold it together.

She tested what looked like the power knob on the radio, frantically turning it back and forth. She pushed the audio button and held her mouth close to the speaker. "This is Chelsea Hammond trying to call the helicopter. Helicopter, do you read me?"

Her voice sounded weak and wobbly. She cleared her throat and tried again after a second of silence.

"This is Chelsea Hammond trying to call the helicopter. Helicopter, do you read me?" She could picture the pilot's stunned expression over the silence. Who was this again?

After a moment, a voice responded. "Chelsea, are you OK?"

"Renner, is that you?"

"Sure is, baby. How are you?"

Was this nightmare close to over? Shaking with

relief, she responded. "We've had a run-in with Jake's dad. Trey's been shot twice. You guys flew directly overhead but apparently didn't see me waving."

"Where are you?"

"I don't really know. Can you follow your path backwards?"

"Chelsea, where's Trey?"

"He's passed out."

"Can you try to rouse him?"

"Hang on. Don't go anywhere. Let me try to wake him." She rolled her eyes. Was she stupid or what? Don't go anywhere? He was in a moving helicopter definitely headed somewhere. Hopefully, back in their direction.

She turned around and tapped Trey gently on his right shoulder, trying to rouse him without hurting him. "Trey. Wake up. I've got the helicopter on the radio."

A single click pierced the silence behind her.

Chelsea didn't have to turn around to know who it was.

How could this be happening to them? To her? A woman whose only goal was to fulfill God's plan for her life by counseling hurting teens. A person who liked her private life secure, even boring.

Why her?

Crouched low to the ground, she slowly angled to face Jake's dad, while her body shielded Trey.

Jake's dad didn't look so good either. Sweat beaded on his greasy forehead. His lips were dry and cracked and an ugly cigar hung from his mouth.

Her hand still clutched Trey's radio. She moved so Carpocelli wouldn't see it and pushed the audio button to record their conversation. Renner would figure it out. If only he could figure out their location before it was too late. She needed to keep Carpocelli talking.

"You have got to be kidding! You're worse than that stupid battery bunny on TV."

"Nope. Not kidding. Not this time. This time you won't be quite so lucky." He coughed when the cigar smoke drifted in front of his nose.

"Lucky? What makes you think I'm lucky? God's taking care of me. And your son needs someone to take care of him. Why aren't you doing that? What kind of example are you setting for him?"

"Shut up. Wake your boyfriend up."

"I can't wake him up. He's hurt. He needs medical attention, just like you do. He's been sleeping for a while now. You wake him up."

"Wake him up, or I'll kill you both right now." His features twisted more grimly. He pointed the gun directly at her.

The man was definitely not kidding.

She nodded and turned back around to Trey, being careful not to use the hand with the radio, which she hoped was still recording their conversation. This was getting serious. "Trey. Wake up. I need your help. Jake's dad is back."

Trey's eyelids fluttered, and his right hand flinched. He thought he still had a gun.

She winced. It was her fault he didn't. Where had she left it?

She tried again, repeating herself more for Renner's benefit than Trey's. "Trey. Wake up. Carpocelli has a gun."

His eyes flickered open, scanned the immediate area, taking in their circumstances. Landed on her. Then Carpocelli.

"What do you want, Carpocelli?"

Trey's voice sounded weak. Where was that helicopter? He needed to get to the hospital. Chelsea scanned the sky.

"You know what I want. But just in case you forgot, I'll remind you. First, I want my son. Where is he?"

"How do you think I would know the answer to that out here?"

Carpocelli's scowl grew fierce. He tossed his cigar into the woods. "You better come up with the answer real quick like or your girlfriend will be the first to go." Carpocelli cocked the gun at Chelsea's head.

Trey's face blanched.

Chelsea gulped and said another prayer.

"I'll find out where Jake is. Let Chelsea go. She doesn't mean anything to you."

"Well now, that's not exactly true. Now is it, Colten?"

"I don't know what you're talking about."

Chelsea winced at Trey's weak voice and ashen face. He needed to get to the hospital pronto. Whatever Carpocelli was ranting about didn't matter right now. Trey's life hung in the balance.

Her finger tightened on the radio's audio button while she scanned the ground searching for the gun. Ah. There it was. On Trey's right side where she had dropped it. She couldn't pick it up now, though. Wait for the best opportunity. Catch Carpocelli off-guard.

Carpocelli grinned. Then, he laughed, a raucous laugh that ended in a coughing fit. His face lost all its mirth. "Why don't we tell *Mrs.* Chelsea Hammond here what she means to you?" He spit out her name as if it were a bad taste in his mouth.

"Trey has been protecting me from you. Because of your violence. And because your own son wants to testify against you." Frustration dripped from her voice. She remembered Jake's sweet, terrified face when she found him in the barn. She would gladly do this all over again to protect him from this monster.

Carpocelli snorted. "Colten, fess up, before I tell her."

"Tell me what?" Chelsea's hand grew clammy on the radio. Trey didn't have much time. Where was that helicopter?

"Chelsea Hammond. Widow of Doug Hammond." Carpocelli sneered. "I know that name rings a bell with you, Colten. It sure did me when I heard it."

26

"You're too late, Carpocelli. Chelsea knows you're the reason her husband is dead." Yeah. He was buying time, trying to find his gun, but he also wanted Chelsea to hear the truth. From someone besides him.

"Well now. Seems to me you're the reason her husband's no longer around. Looks like you moved in and took his place right slick there, marshal."

If Trey could have gotten up, he would have punched that sneer off Carpocelli's face.

"Stop it!" Chelsea screamed, shaking her head back and forth at Carpocelli. Tears sprouted from those voluminous green eyes. "Get out. Leave us alone."

Trey wanted so badly to take her in his arms, to comfort her. But, she wouldn't want comfort from him anytime soon. Carpocelli had gotten the better of him, crippling him for the rest of his life. That is, if he made it out of here alive. A big if.

The helicopter's blades sounded directly overhead. Carpocelli's head jerked towards the sound. Knowing he would only have the briefest window of opportunity, Trey reached for his gun.

Carpocelli must have realized his few days of freedom were about to be cut short because he took off.

"Carpocelli. Give it up. Drop the gun," Trey yelled after him.

Carpocelli continued slinking through the woods.

Trey moaned. He couldn't do much with a wounded arm and leg. But he wasn't going to let him get away, to continue terrorizing sweet people like Jake and Chelsea. Killing innocent people like Doug. He'd give it everything he had left to send this scum to the slammer for life. Even if it meant his own.

He could lure Carpocelli back if Chelsea was out of the way.

"Chelsea, I need you to follow the helicopter that way. Don't stop until you make it to the chopper." Trey winced at the compassion lining Chelsea's face, the tears streaming down her face.

He didn't want her pity. Or her sympathy. He wanted her love.

There wasn't much he could do about that now. It wasn't the time or the place. He had to stop this guy.

"Go!" he screamed. "Now."

She jumped. He waited for a second and watched her, cradling his wounded left arm with his other hand, until he saw her follow his orders, her tears still flowing. She kept looking back at him, sadness brimming.

Trey's heart lurched, thoughts of his promise pricking his conscious. He'd never be able to come through with that kiss.

But he couldn't worry about that now. Worrying would only take his mind from what he needed to do. Which was forcing Carpocelli to surrender. Trey made his way to his feet, found a stick to use as a cane.

He shuffled a few feet in Carpocelli's direction, made sure Chelsea was nowhere in sight. "Carpocelli, you coward, come back here," he hollered. Trey stood, swaying slightly, waiting. "You want to kill me, don't you? Now's your chance."

Carpocelli stepped into view.

One shot. That's probably all Trey had in him.

Please God.

Trey clipped off a shot, nicking the gun out of Carpocelli's hand. Not quite where he was aiming, but at least he'd disabled the slug. "I want to see your face on the ground. Face on the ground. Both hands spread out where I can see them."

Hatred and evil seeped out of Carpocelli's eyes before he complied with Trey's request and flopped to the ground. But there was that ever present grin on his face...

The slime ball who had haunted his dreams for the last three years lay on the ground at his feet.

The one who had invaded his thoughts every waking hour for the last three years.

The one who should be suffering in prison but ran wild and free, wreaking havoc.

And the one who had probably ruined every fighting chance he had with the woman he loved.

Now was his big chance to take Carpocelli out for good. So that Carpocelli could never hurt his own son again. Or Chelsea. It was too late for Trey.

No one would be the wiser.

He leveled his gun at Carpocelli's back.

৵৵৵

Chelsea ran after the helicopter. She'd gotten them both in enough trouble already by not listening to Trey. This time she was obeying orders.

Even if she didn't like them.

She ran right into Ethan and Jamee. Jamee pulled her into her arms and patted her back while Chelsea sobbed. "I've never...been...so happy...to see two...of my friends...in my life."

They represented safety. Security. Home. She shuddered. Carpocelli was still out there. She'd never be safe until...

Jamee held Chelsea at arm's length. "Chelsea, you're OK?"

Chelsea nodded, shaking, clinging to her friend. "I'm alive. I'm not the one who's hurt. Trey is. Carpocelli shot him. Twice. Once in the arm and once in the leg. He's bleeding badly, but he wouldn't let me stay with him. He ordered me to follow the helicopter. I think he was planning on tracking him down."

Confusion clouded Ethan's features. She could relate. "Trey took off after Carpocelli? Or the other way around?"

"I'm not sure what Trey had planned, Ethan. Trey told me to follow the helicopter, but I saw him trying to stand up. I think he was going after Carpocelli. But Carpocelli is also wounded. In the leg."

"Renner is tracking them down. You guys have been busy," Ethan said.

"What took the helicopter so long?"

"Hamilton gave orders for the chopper to transport Jake out of the area first. He didn't want to take any chances that Carpocelli might have somebody else snatch him while he diverted their attention."

"That was a good idea. I wouldn't put it past Carpocelli. That man is pure evil." Chelsea shivered, reliving the ordeal of the past few hours. The memories of this day would haunt her for years, not only because of Carpocelli's actions, but also because of his words.

"We followed the chopper, Chelsea, with the SUV. So we can take you to the hospital now if you want,"

Jamee said, patting Chelsea's back.

Chelsea shook her head, unable to dam the tears flowing down her cheeks. "I'm going with Trey to the hospital. I'm not sure he's going to make it."

☙ ❧

Don't do this, my son. I will take care of this. I AM enough for you.

Trey heard the voice as if it were whispered directly in his ear. He looked around, but didn't see anybody. Didn't matter. Trey knew Who spoke the whispered words.

Trey lowered his gaze and his gun. He couldn't do it. He had to bring Carpocelli in. No matter how he felt personally about the sleaze ball, he couldn't pull the trigger. God would take care of him.

He moved towards Carpocelli.

Trey picked up the movement a second too late. Carpocelli rolled on the ground and came up holding his gun, aimed straight at him.

He heard a blast come from somewhere behind him and through his fog saw Carpocelli's form thud backwards with a look of finality. Trey collapsed on the ground.

"You may not have wanted to pull that trigger, Trey, but I sure did. I'm glad he gave me an excuse." Renner's voice sounded distant somewhere from behind. Suddenly, he was kneeling on the ground next to him. "Where are you hurt, buddy?"

"Everywhere," Trey complained. "He got me on the arm and the leg."

"Whoa. Why didn't you take him out while you had the chance?" Renner asked, surprised.

"I don't know, Renner. I guess God had other plans," Trey whispered before losing consciousness.

27

"Hey, partner. Thought you were going to make a week of it," Renner said, folding the newspaper in half.

"How long was I out?" Sandpaper gritted Trey's throat.

"An entire day with lots of moaning and groaning. Oh, and by the way, has anybody ever told you that you talk in your sleep?"

Renner was needling him. He decided to play along. "Oh yeah? What was I saying?"

"You kept saying 'I am enough. I am enough.' What were you referring to?"

Maybe Renner wasn't teasing him. He remembered hearing those words somewhere in his subconscious, kept replaying the voice in his head.

"Who."

"What do you mean, who?"

"God."

"God? How does God fit into this?"

"Can I explain it to you when I'm feeling a little better?"

"Sure, buddy." Renner smiled. "You've had a constant visitor. I finally convinced her to go home and catch a little sleep."

He moaned, remembering her tears, the pity in her gaze when she looked at him in the helicopter. Remembered losing consciousness with her gentle fingers rubbing his forehead, breathing close to his ear. "Hang on, honey. Hang on." Probably the only thing that kept him here, the fact that she'd called him honey.

Renner chuckled. "Yep. You were talking in your sleep. Wouldn't have anything to do with a beautiful red-headed school counselor, now would it?"

Trey closed his eyes. What should he do? Did he want her to see him like this? Would she want him if he couldn't walk? Could they have a life together with Doug between them?

So many questions made his head pound. He cradled his forehead with a hand. "Do you think you could get a pain-killer for me? My head is throbbing."

Renner looked sheepish as he rang for the nurse. "Sure. I'm sorry, man. I didn't mean to bring up a sore subject."

"That's all right. I'm sure it's just from the injuries. And an ego issue." Trey forced a weak smile. "Thanks for being my partner. And for being there when I needed it. Sorry you had to come in and save the day for me."

Renner shook his head. "Oh no. Believe me, that was my pleasure. Carpocelli isn't around to haunt us anymore. They pronounced him dead on scene." He paused for a second. "He won't be around to cause any more pain. Not to Jake, to you, or to Chelsea."

Trey closed his eyes briefly to savor that thought, but then felt remorse that the man chose evil over God. He opened his eyes, took a deep breath. "So what's the scoop on Jake?"

"I think you'll have to hear that from the horse's mouth." Renner laughed.

Trey frowned. He must already have some

painkillers in his system. Understanding this conversation was taking a toll on him. He closed his eyes.

"Hey, I've been thinking. Maybe it's time you settled down. Got married."

Trey opened his eyes slowly. Marriage was probably the last thing on his agenda right now. *Be truthful, Trey.* OK, so he had been thinking about it. A lot. But now? Facing the prospect of never walking again?

"Renner, I don't want Chelsea here." He looked down at his leg and almost choked on his words. "Not like this."

Renner's face fell. "You can't be serious."

Trey nodded. "Yeah. I am. Keep her out, would you?" He dropped his head back on the pillow, allowed his eyelids to close again. "I'm kind of tired. I think I need some more rest."

"Sure. I'll go take care of some business and come by later. Now that you're back with the living."

❧

"Chelsea. I'm sorry. I know he doesn't mean it. He's just scared." Renner's voice knifed through Chelsea's heart.

She'd regret forever leaving his side to catch a few hours of sleep. Now she wouldn't be able to sift her hand through his hair, to trail her fingers along his scar, to whisper words of encouragement in his ears. She wanted to be there for Trey, to bear this pain with him, to help him recover. To shower him with forgiveness and her love.

And now he was shutting her out. Slamming the

door. Just like that. Because he was scared? A former Marine? A marshal who battled thugs like Carpocelli every day?

Scared?

The wind howled outside the kitchen window. The grey clouds she woke to a few minutes earlier churned and swirled. She wrapped arms around her chest, feeling a chill inside her heart.

Chelsea stared at the tea kettle on the stove. Snuggles nuzzled her leg. "What is he scared of, Renner? Doug?"

Chelsea turned off the burner and poured the hot water into mugs. She placed their mugs on the counter and sat down at the bar. She heaved a huge sigh. "Or scared about us?"

"I think he's scared about not walking again."

She sent him an agonized look. "You know whether he ever walks again or not has nothing to do with how I feel about him. The fact that he's in this position is my fault to begin with."

"None of this is your fault, Chelsea. Give him time. He'll come around. How can he not?" Renner's gentle smile did little to soothe her nerves.

"How can he not?" She scoffed and brushed an errant curl behind her ear. "I guess he could just give up on the whole situation, thinking I'm too much trouble, too much headache. And now with Jake..."

Renner nodded, his eyes bright. "That's exactly what I'm talking about. You're such a giving, caring person, Chelsea. Trey can't help but see through his fear to find his way back to you. He just needs a little time to sort things out, put things in perspective."

She wrapped hands around the mug, staring down at the hot tea and frowned. OK. She'd give Trey the time he needed to process his thoughts, sort out his feelings. But she didn't have to like it. She wanted to be with him. They'd both suffered too long, too much. It was time for it all to be over.

"OK, Renner. He knows where to find me. I'll be here. Waiting for him."

28

"Stop."

At Jake's uplifted hand, Chelsea mashed the brake pedal, shifted the truck into PARK, and stepped out. "Thanks, Jake. Do you want to help me get the horses into their stalls?" Her home had been Jake's home for a full month since his father's death. Although he loosened up more every day, he still hesitated staying outside for any length of time.

"Do you need help?" His pasty look said it all.

"It's OK. I'm fine with just two. But I will need more help this weekend when we go pick up the other six."

"OK then. See you inside." Jake opened the door of the truck to grab his book bag and sling it over his shoulder.

"I've got some brownies with your name on them in the kitchen."

That garnered a smile from him. "Thanks, Chelsea."

Chelsea walked around to the back of the trailer and put her gloves on. She led both horses, Colten and Renner, to their stalls and made sure they had fresh water. Looping her arms over Colten's stall door, she just stared. She couldn't help herself. He was a beauty.

Thank you, God.

She heard a scuffling noise behind her. Jake must

have changed his mind about helping her.

"I heard you might have a housekeeper position available."

She sucked in a breath. That deep voice didn't belong to Jake.

"I might." She turned around. Slowly. She wanted a good, long look at the man who held her heart in his hands.

Where was his monogrammed shirt? The one with *Deputy U.S. Marshal* emblazoned on the front? Even without the monogrammed shirt, he looked scrumptious in jeans and a black t-shirt. His hair reached to the top of his shirt, and he hadn't shaved in days. The cane at his right side only added to his allure. But that meant she couldn't run and jump into his arms...

"But I have to tell you, up front, I don't work well with marshals. I can't seem to follow directions very well..." Her lips curved, she tilted her head sideways to gauge his response.

"I guess it's a good thing I don't work for them anymore." Trey grinned and lifted his cane in the air. "Disability."

What? Renner hadn't told her that. She took her gloves off and hung them up. "Kalyn's parents finally wised up and asked her to move back home, so I do need a housekeeper. But I know that can't be why you're here."

Pain radiated from his eyes. "I owe you an apology, one you probably don't want to hear but one I owe, anyway. Can we go sit down on the porch? This leg doesn't let me stand too long at one time right now."

Every day and night for four weeks, she had

prayed about this minute. Was she ready? *God help me here. Give me the right words to let him know how I feel. Help me not to be a coward.* She summoned her strongest voice. "OK."

She walked over to stand next to him. When she felt his free hand find the small of her back, she almost caved and threw her arms around him. But he needed to do this more than she needed to hear it. She led him to the back deck and motioned for him to sit in her favorite spot.

"Would you like some coffee?"

He reached into his jacket pocket and pulled out some antacids, studied the roll, and then placed it back in his pocket, unopened. "No. I need to get this off my chest. Coffee won't make it any easier. Or me any less nervous."

Chelsea nodded. "OK. Shoot." She scrunched her eyes, mentally chastising herself for the choice of words.

She looked directly into his eyes. She wanted him to see the depths of her forgiveness, the width of her love.

"'I'm sorry' doesn't begin to cover everything. Sorry about Doug, about your baby—"

She couldn't stand it anymore. Couldn't allow him to carry this guilt any longer. She got out of her seat and knelt in front of him, covered each one of his hands with hers. "Trey. Had the situation been reversed and Doug had worked on that case for years, I know he would have made the same choice. You made what you thought was the best choice. And, after what Carpocelli put me through in just one day, I would have also made the same choice you did. In a heartbeat."

Trey lifted tormented eyes to look at her. "What are you saying?"

"I forgive you. Just like God has forgiven me for nailing his Son to the cross, I forgive you. Now the only thing left is for you to forgive yourself."

She might as well go for the gusto here. Bare her feelings on her sleeve. "Does your girlfriend know how special you are?"

He looked confused. "My girlfriend?"

Renner was right. He didn't have a girlfriend. He'd been talking about her. "The one you said you found, but it wasn't the right time and that if you couldn't have her, you didn't want anybody."

The twinkle reemerged in his eyes. He pulled her up to sit on his good leg. "Mmmm. I don't know about that. But I do know one thing. I want my girlfriend to know how special she is." He ran his hand through her hair, gently pulled at one of her curls.

"I love you, Chelsea Hammond. I love the way you care about people, about teenagers, about animals. I want to spend every day for the rest of my life waking up to your curls tickling my forehead and kissing those freckles that refuse to be covered up. I want to listen to you sing and play your guitar. I want to enjoy life with you. I want to grow old with you."

Trey's eyes crinkled at the corners and his lips curved upwards, teasing. "It would be nice, though, if every once in a while you would follow directions. Simple directions, like not standing next to an open window when a mobster is on the prowl."

Chelsea grinned. "Follow directions? What's the fun in all that? If I had, I might have missed that heart-curling, knee-knocking tackle of yours! You have to take the good with the bad, you know." She wrapped her arms around his neck and softened her voice. "So, are you ready to be a parent?"

"Is that a proposal?"

She giggled and thumped his chest.

His eyes darkened, and he lowered his head, his breath fanning her lips. "I made a promise to you, and I intend to keep it."

Her lips parted. "A promise?" she whispered.

He leaned closer. "Yeah. Did you forget?"

She'd been waiting so long for this. For him. She shook her head, hardly daring to breathe. "How could I forget a kiss like yours?"

She closed her eyes and lifted her face. He kissed her. And this time he didn't stop until she pulled back for air. This time, his kiss was full of promise. Full of love and commitment.

He feathered her nose with another kiss. He circled both arms around her, cradling her to his chest. She sighed and didn't even attempt to control her hands that had taken to playing with the hair sticking out from his shirt.

"I certainly wouldn't want you to experience the empty nest syndrome when Jake leaves for college in four years. I want the house full of teenagers. And babies," Trey added.

Chelsea gasped, and then narrowed her eyes, forgetting for a minute the hair on his chest. "Renner said he wasn't going to tell you."

"He kept his promise. And because he refused to tell me, I made an educated guess. A young man who just lost both parents in such a violent way? I knew you wouldn't pass up the opportunity staring you in the face no matter who it was. I was hoping for the same for me." He drew his head closer, caressed her with another soft kiss. "Chelsea, I know we can't make up for the baby God chose to take home so soon, but we can fill the house with babies and teenagers to love and cherish. Just like I cherish you."

He closed his eyes, and his grip around her tightened. "Can you love me even if I never ditch the cane?"

Chelsea couldn't stop the tear from sliding down her cheek. She reached up and gripped his face with both her hands until he opened his eyes and could see the love radiating from her own. "I love you just the way you are. Cane or no cane. Beard or no beard. Deputy U.S. Marshal or not."

The tenseness left his arms. "I've applied for my Private Investigator's license. No more traveling for me. I'm home for good." He paused and reached into his pocket. "I've got something for you."

She took the tiny pieces of paper he offered. Five tickets to a big car race in Tennessee!

Chelsea grinned and planted a kiss on his lips.

"Aren't you going to see where it is?"

"It doesn't matter. I'll go."

"That's good to know. But I think you better check the date. Make sure you don't have any other commitments."

He sure knew the way into her heart. She looked to see when the race was, wrinkled her eyebrows when she couldn't find the date. The date had been replaced with a word. The first ticket said, "Will." She flipped it over and glanced at the second. "You."

What?

The third said, "Marry" and the fourth...

She gasped and met his eyes.

He pulled her gently from his lap and guided her

to sit in the chair while he bent down on his good knee. "I meant what I said. I want to spend forever with you, Chelsea. Will you marry me?"

"Yes."

Chelsea closed her eyes and allowed Trey's kiss to penetrate her heart.

God was good all the time. He'd helped her keep her vow never to fall in love with a law enforcement officer again. She'd never mentioned PIs in her prayers...

Epilogue

Three o'clock. June tenth. But no mystery man with haunted eyes waited for her this year.

No. This year was better. Her husband and son waited for her.

Chelsea stopped at Henry's car and turned around. Leaning against the open bed of the truck with his arms crossed and a smile tugging at his lips, Trey listened to Jake's story while Snuggles slept in the truck bed. Jake's face lit up, his hands moved a mile a minute.

Trey always teased Jake about talking with his hands. *If he couldn't talk with his hands, he wouldn't talk at all.*

Trey's gaze slanted her way, and he flashed a grin before turning his attention back to Jake.

She smiled. She loved her guys.

"Nice family you have there," Henry commented, following her gaze. "I'm happy for you."

"Thanks, Henry." She wrapped her arms around his frail body for a hug. "I'm so sorry about Stella."

"Thank you, dear. Life isn't the same without our loved ones. But God is good, isn't He? He'll help me heal in time. Just like He did for you." Henry patted her back and then pulled away with a twinkle lighting his eyes. "I'm glad to see you with a smile in your heart this year, not just on your face."

Chelsea's hand rubbed her budding abdomen.

Oh, yeah. God is good.